• The •
MEIJI
PRINCE

Adam Anthony

Portland • Oregon
inkwaterpress.com

Copyright © 2013 by Adam Anthony

Cover and interior design by Masha Shubin

Old Map of Japan © Pontus Edenberg. DreamsTime.com
Samurai Sword © Darren Whittingham. BigStockPhoto.com

This is a work of fiction. The events described here are imaginary. The settings and characters are fictitious or used in a fictitious manner and do not represent specific places or living or dead people. Any resemblance is entirely coincidental.

All rights reserved. No part of this book may be reproduced or transmitted in any form or by any means whatsoever, including photocopying, recording or by any information storage and retrieval system, without written permission from the publisher and/or author. Contact Inkwater Press at 6750 SW Franklin Street, Suite A, Portland, OR 97223-2542. 503.968.6777

Publisher: Inkwater Press | www.inkwaterpress.com

Paperback
ISBN-13 978-1-59299-903-3 | ISBN-10 1-59299-903-4

Printed in the U.S.A.
All paper is acid free and meets all ANSI standards for archival quality paper.

1 3 5 7 9 10 8 6 4 2

ONE

There he is again, Hamish thought, as he caught a glimpse from the corner of his eye of the well-dressed Oriental gentleman who was peering into the small display window of his photography studio on Market Street – for the third time in a week.

On those previous occasions, as soon as Hamish went to the door, in order to engage the gentleman in conversation and possibly lure him into the studio for a portrait sitting, the mysterious stranger rushed off – appearing to be embarrassed? Frightened?

This time, however, Hamish was determined to avoid scaring off his prey. He pretended to not see him, as he walked through the curtain, in the far wall of the studio – which separated it from his darkroom, and then through the single room where he lived behind the studio.

He opened the back door leading into the alley and walked past the rear of the two shops closest to his. At the end of the alley, he turned the corner quietly and soon was standing next to the startled gentleman. It was *too* late now for the latter to rush off again.

Hamish smiled at the man, who nervously touched the buttons on his well-tailored black suit jacket, and also the brim of his hat, several times.

Hamish pointed to the display window, filled with

portraits, carte-de-visité, and a few modest porcelain objects purchased at a nearby street market, to make the window display appear less monotonous, more homelike.

"Please, Sir" he pleaded, "come inside and let me show you more of my work."

The gentleman bowed stiffly from the waist, arms straight by his sides, and slowly followed Hamish into the studio. Inside, Hamish made a gesture toward the most-comfortable chair in the studio – the one favored by ladies who came in adorned in the latest 1874-version of stylish fancy dress in San Francisco.

"Would you care for some coffee?" Hamish inquired, ready to retrieve the brew which sat for most of the day atop the pot-bellied stove in his living quarters.

"No, thank you," the visitor responded, in slightly British-accented English. This brief exchange reflected the fact that because Hamish had such limited experience with persons from the Orient, despite his having lived in San Francisco for so many years, he was unfamiliar with their preference for *tea*.

He then brought forth several portraits of local merchants, in their Sunday-best, as they were closest in appearance to the formal garb of his mysterious visitor. The latter studied them intently, while he appeared to be gradually relaxing and losing some of the nervous gestures which had characterized his behavior from the first time Hamish spotted him peering in the window.

"Do you have any photographs of *landscapes* I may examine," he asked Hamish, after a time.

Hamish went to a nearby storage cabinet and retrieved several photographs he had taken along the waterfront and in local parks, and handed them to his guest.

Upon viewing them, the gentleman smiled – for the first time. He then stared at Hamish intently for what appeared to be a very long time, making Hamish nervous *now*. The Westerner before him was of average height (for an American!), blue-eyed, with a light-colored blond mustache and a head of thick blond hair. His complexion had the pallor associated with labor that was largely indoors. Finally, he spoke.

"The sign on your door says you are *Mr. Boyd?*"

"*Hamish* Boyd. And you, Sir?"

"Forgive me, Mr. Boyd, for not introducing myself sooner. I am Mr. Edo Hasegawa – I am a staff member at the Japanese Consulate here in San Francisco."

"I didn't know you folks had a Consulate here, Mr. Hasegawa," Hamish responded.

"Oh yes, since 1860, after my country opened itself to the West and the *Treaty of Amity and Commerce* with the United States was signed by our nations several years earlier. Now, with the modern ocean-going steamships operating regularly between here and Yokohama, there is much travel and commerce between our countries."

"I know the Chinese are around these here parts – came over in large numbers as laborers mostly, but I didn't know lots of Japanese were here," Hamish said, offhandedly. And then without intentional malice, he added, "I really can't tell the difference between them, you know, all Orientals....."

Hamish's voice suddenly trailed off, as he became acutely aware how insulting he might be appearing to this representative of the Japanese Consulate.

For his part, Edo Hasegawa maintained the

expressionless face endemic in diplomatic circles, and continued with his well-rehearsed story.

"I am here on commission of a member of the Imperial Family back in Edo – I mean to say, *Tokyo*. His name is Prince Kashiwara. He is engaged in commerce and has a printing factory which currently specializes in selling souvenir woodcuts to local residents and, increasingly, to foreign tourists – the steamship service, you understand."

"Yes, Sir. But why did he hire you – I mean *commission* you?"

"Prince Kashiwara believes that the Western invention of the camera has changed everything, making woodcuts increasingly obsolete. He thus wishes to convert his business to that of providing souvenir photographs, instead. In view of that decision, he has asked me to engage someone here to go to Japan and teach him and his staff the skills necessary for taking and producing photographs, for commercial purposes."

"Begging your pardon, but I'm not quite sure where I come into this," Hamish replied, somewhat perplexed by this unexpected visitor's message.

"I have examined your work several times, in the display window – sometimes at night when your studio was closed for the day. And after seeing more of your efforts today, I believe it is superior to that of others I viewed in the City – despite the *humble* nature of your premises. Oh, do forgive me, I did not mean to be rude with my words."

"No need to apologize, Sir. Truth be told, I am flattered."

Hasegawa continued. "The Prince needs someone to come to Japan for six months – actually one month will be spent traveling each way, and four months working there. Your salary would be paid monthly for the entire period, and your transportation also provided. Here is the proposed salary I am authorized to offer."

Hamish took the proffered small piece of paper from Hasegawa's outstretched hand and tried to conceal his shock and delight at the compensation being offered.

"I am mighty graveled, Mr. Hasegawa! This is a whole lot to consider, coming at me so sudden-like. I woke up this morning thinking I'd be in this shop – or maybe a bigger one, all my life. I didn't expect an offer to go traipsing off to a foreign land."

Edo Hasegawa was unfamiliar with much of the working-class slang widely in use in San Francisco at the time, and had no idea what *graveled* and *traipsing* meant, but continued on with the remaining crucial details of the offer.

"Actually, the Prince is quite anxious for you to travel soon. I can give you but three days at the most to give me your decision – either way. And then, if you agree to accept, I must start making the travel arrangements – to coincide with the ship's sailing schedule, you understand."

"Hugger-mugger! Three days to decide? That's mighty short! Even if I decide to go, there is the problem of what to do with my studio here – I have a lease."

"I am truly sorry I must ask for such a quick decision, but the Prince is most adamant for a prompt resolution of this matter. And if I may say, speaking frankly, one in my position dare not disappoint a member of the Imperial Family."

"I reckon I see the fix you are in, Sir. Three days?

Alright, in three days I will let you know my decision. How do I contact you?"

Mr. Hasegawa reached into the breast pocket of his jacket and withdrew a carte-de-visite, containing his photograph and contact information at the Consulate. Then, realizing this was a photographic service Hamish Boyd *could* have provided, he quickly added, "My Superior at the Consulate obtained these calling cards for *all* his staff – we did not individually purchase them."

Hamish laughed at this point. "I realize there's more than one photographer in San Francisco, Mr. Hasegawa, and am mighty flattered you have made this important offer to *me*."

Edo Hasegawa faked a smile, inwardly uncomfortable that it was necessary to conceal the fact that he had offered two other local photographers the commission *first* – but each had declined due to family obligations which would keep them in San Francisco. He then rose, and once again bowed stiffly, before Hamish could extend his hand, and walked to the door.

"I shall see you in three days at the Consulate, Mr. Boyd."

"Yep, you will, Sir."

TWO

After Mr. Hasegawa left, Hamish found himself unable to concentrate on his work. His mind was racing with thoughts of the offer he had received so unexpectedly that day, and the need for a decision in but three days.

Eventually, he gave up and hung the *CLOSED* sign on his studio door, dimmed the lamps, and retired to his single-room residence at the back of the building.

He poured himself a cup of coffee and sat in his old rocking chair, furiously propelling himself back and forth – to no purpose.

After a time, he rose and went to retrieve the glass jar where he stored his meager earnings until those rare occasions when he had accumulated a profit which could be taken to his neighborhood bank for deposit.

As he counted the contents of the jar, he realized he had enough, with a bit more to spare, to make an early visit to the bordello where he *relieved* himself monthly. They would not be expecting him until next week, but would still be more than happy to take his hard-earned cash anyway.

And so, he made his way to Morton Street, in the Barbary Coast neighborhood – one replete with brothels which served working-class men such as him.

The *Madam* was noticeably surprised to see him, but assured him his favorite, *Maisie*, would be free shortly, and would he like a bit of whiskey while waiting?

Of course, the latter query was all a ruse, enacted by the Madam upon *every* visitor – in order to increase her takings from gentleman callers before they went to *the rooms*.

Hamish knew well the ploy, and had budgeted for a single whiskey that day. And as soon as he finished his drink, by coincidence, Maisie was now *free*.

Nothing had changed in the appearance of Maisie's room since he first entered it and lost his virginity there not long after his arrival in San Francisco a dozen years earlier, at the age of eighteen.

Maisie was also of a tender age at that time – and neither was yet jaded by the repetitious, routine, impersonal nature of purchased intimacy. But now, Maisie looked much older, and appeared more tired and silent than in those early years – but she still always managed to flash a smile in Hamish's direction when he entered, and later left, her room.

For some reason, during *this* visit, Hamish was more-acutely aware of his surroundings than in the past. His photographer's eye for detail had previously taken second place to concentration on the act to be performed. But on this day, as he and Maisie went through the motions of thrust and re-thrust, he found himself focusing on the tawdry bedcovers, faded window curtains, and peeling wallpaper.

When his release eventually came, it brought no joy – just a bit of *relief* from the stress he felt since Mr. Hasegawa's visit and surprise offer. And as he walked out the door moments later, he realized that he could have achieved the same results today, using his own hand, in the privacy of his room – while preserving his hard-earned cash as well!

Now, he was despondent, as well as stressed and confused as to which way to turn at this time. He noticed a rustic bench in a small, untidy park and sat down to think a bit on matters before going back to his stuffy, little room. A room, he realized, barely a notch above Maisie's tawdry quarters.

Routine! Yes, routine was the hallmark of his life, now. At the age of thirty he was clearly locked into a routine existence, until the day he died.

His loving father had stressed the value of seeking and accepting routine, and the promise of a steady livelihood and a quiet, uneventful life that was likely to follow.

Growing up poor, but with the chance to attend a one-room schoolhouse until he was twelve, his father absorbed his lessons in reading, writing and arithmetic – and thus, at that tender age was put to work in a local general store. Over time, he was promoted steadily and eventually became the highly-visible Manager of one such establishment in the Santa Rosa area.

And then, in the 1850s, when Wells Fargo established an Outpost and General Store in Santa Rosa, he was tapped to manage it for that prestigious organization. Hamish was just a young lad at the time, but his father made certain he attended the local school and learned his *three-Rs*, also.

But beyond the focus upon a solid education in the basic skills, his father also stressed – both at home and in the store where Hamish helped out, the need to be polite, courteous, and well-spoken when dealing with the public. In an era when desperate, rough-and-tumble characters were pouring into California to seek their mythic fortunes, his father wanted Hamish to stand apart. And Hamish did absorb these values so well, that his demeanor and earnestness eventually attracted someone who would alter the course of his young life.

Several times each year, an itinerant photographer from San Francisco came to the Wells Fargo Outpost and took photographs of local residents. His wagon, outfitted as a darkroom, fascinated Hamish from the first time it appeared – a place where a mysterious process created magical results on paper. He quizzed the gentleman so often over the years, about photography, that when he was eighteen years old, the man presented a proposition to Hamish's father.

He was getting old, he told him, and wanted to apprentice a young man who could acquire his skills and hopefully lease his studio back in San Francisco when he retired. At one and the same time, Hamish would learn a skill in order to provide for himself, and the old photographer would have a steady retirement income from the lease.

Soon, Hamish was on his way to San Francisco, with his father's blessing, and there he apprenticed to the gentleman until the latter retired not long thereafter, not in the best of health. But now, a dozen years later, as he sat in this untidy, over-grown little park, evaluating his present and future – he fully realized he had fallen into the routine existence his father promised, but which he now felt was suffocating him. *Routine!* Was this all his life was to be from now until death?

Mr. Hasegawa, ironically, had offered an unexpected alternative – to go on an adventure to a mysterious, distant, land for half a year. This was an opportunity never anticipated – was it not to be fulfilled because of fear? indecisiveness? loss of youthful exuberance, hope and adventure?

No! Hamish concluded, as he quickly rose from the rotting bench. *I must seize this opportunity at all costs, for such as this may never come my way again! But how to do that?*

And then, on the walk back to his studio, a plan began to slowly form in his mind. He too had apprenticed a young man recently – one eager to pay a small (but welcome) fee to learn the mysteries of modern photography, and as far as Hamish knew, the lad was still in need of the opportunity to exercise his new profession, while working at the harbor, loading bales onto ships.

Perhaps, Hamish thought, *there is an easy resolution to the problem of maintaining my lease during my absence!*

THREE

Three days later, Hamish stood before the heavy carved door, to the right of which was a wall-mounted sign in Japanese characters – with the English words, *Consulate of Japan, San Francisco*, written below.

With his right hand he grasped the large brass knocker and struck it several times against the matching metal plate affixed to the door. In his left hand he held his carte-de-visite.

The door was soon opened by a small Asian gentleman, dressed in a simple black suit. He bowed stiffly to Hamish, and upon seeing the carte-de-visite Hamish was offering in his extended hand, quickly retrieved a small silver tray from a nearby hall commode. Hamish placed the card on the tray and the man bowed again, after which he ushered Hamish into the Consulate's apparent Reception Hall.

Once there, he gestured for Hamish to sit upon an ornately-carved bench, before bowing one more time and leaving the area with the small silver tray in hand.

While he waited, Hamish made a visual inspection of the Hall. He had expected to see *Asian* furnishings in this place, but instead they were neither Oriental nor of the popular American Victorian style currently favored in so many of San Francisco's illustrious homes and offices.

Instead, the elaborate and obviously-expensive furniture appeared to be largely *British*, and of the highest quality. The only items indicating he was in the *Japanese* Consulate were several *objet d'art* in that Nation's style – placed upon a nearby large commode, along with a painted scroll hung on the wall above it. The scene depicted on the latter was quite serene – a lone man fishing by a lake with a bamboo pole, painted in soft pastel colors. *Perhaps it refers to all the fishing in San Francisco Bay*, Hamish decided.

Soon, the gentleman who had received him initially, returned. After another stiff bow, he gestured for Hamish to follow him. Momentarily, the visitor found himself in Mr. Hasegawa's office. As Hasegawa rose from behind his large, elaborate desk, Hamish quickly surveyed the room visually and realized it was also furnished in the highest late-18th-century styles he had seen in several museums where he had been allowed to take some interior photographs.

After he made an awkward attempt to bow in return, when Hasegawa greeted him thusly, he was invited to sit in a chair opposite the latter's desk.

"So," Hasegawa began, "I assume you have made your decision?"

"Yes, Sir. I will be mighty glad to accept your offer!"

Showing little facial emotion, his host replied, "I am most pleased. And so will be Prince Kashiwara. I shall telegraph him of your decision today."

"Telegraph?" Hamish responded, surprised such a feat was possible between San Francisco and Tokyo.

"Japan has had telegraph service for several years now, both domestic and international," Hasegawa clarified.

"That's mighty surprising," Hamish responded. "I thought the steamship service between here and there was a bit of a miracle when you told me about it – but telegraph service too?"

"Oh, yes, Mr. Boyd – you will find much from the West is now at play in my country, once you arrive. Westernization is the highest priority of *Emperor Meiji*."

"Well, I'm flummoxed," Hamish said in response, with a small laugh intended to cover his embarrassment over how naïve he was regarding his upcoming host nation.

Hasegawa continued. "May I ask, what made you decide in our favor, on such short notice?"

"I recently apprenticed a young man who, upon learning my skills, was not yet able to set up his own studio. He has since been doing day work at the docks, and will gladly take over my lease while I am gone."

"I see. So you will be free to leave soon for Japan?"

"Well, Sir – how soon?"

"Two weeks," Hasegawa responded, rather emphatically. "In anticipation of your acceptance, I took the liberty to contact the Captain of the steamship the Consulate uses for our Staff, and he has space for you on the voyage departing two weeks from today. You will arrive in Yokohama in twenty-four days, if the weather remains favorable during your voyage. On the day that you leave here, I am to telegraph Prince Kashiwara you are on your way."

"Two weeks! That's mighty soon. I'll have to quickly get my man in for some review work under my supervision and re-acquaint him with the studio operation, my living quarters, and where to promptly make the leasing payments each month."

"Do you anticipate any problems, Mr. Boyd?"

"No.....guess not. I just didn't reckon things

would move so fast. Now I must give thought to what to take with me."

"Oh, yes – in that regard," Hasegawa interrupted, "the Captain advised me you will only be allowed to carry *two* small trunks onboard."

"*Two* trunks?" Hamish exclaimed, more loudly than the formal, quiet ambiance of this august setting required. "How will I tote all my supplies and my personal goods, for so long a stay?"

"Your supplies – we must talk about *them*. The ship's Captain needs assurance nothing you will be bringing onboard is dangerous. Are your photographic supplies at risk of burning?"

Hamish furrowed his brow, and then composed himself. "Of course, Sir – I use the *wet collodion process*, and the collodion solution is mighty inflammable and can be explosive."

"Is there any other process you can use?" Hasegawa asked, *still* not exhibiting distress on his bland face.

"Not at this time, Sir. There are experiments being done on a *dry plate process*, which would not involve having to coat glass plates with collodion, but we are told its general use is still five, maybe six, years away."

"I see. Well, Prince Kashiwara also apparently anticipated this problem as well. He therefore directed me to inform whoever accepted his offer, that several years ago, a photographic studio was opened in Tokyo by Mr. Kusakabe Kimbei and a German – Baron von Stillfried. They introduced my people to this Western phenomenon and now it is becoming so popular among local persons and tourists, that an astute businessman such as the Prince wishes to duplicate their efforts and even compete with them. As a result, *another* enterprising gentleman, in Yokohama, has established a firm which manufactures the solution and other supplies you will need. And in fact, in the same telegram I am to send when you set sail, I am to include your list of required supplies. In that way, you will have all you need to begin training the Prince's staff immediately upon your arrival. Will you therefore make such a list before you leave here today?"

Hamish was now much relieved. He could fit his meager wardrobe into one small trunk, and his carefully-wrapped precious camera and folding tripod into the other.

"Yes, Sir. I can make a list for you before I leave."

"Fine. I shall send one of our Consulate Staff to the ship's Captain, to finalize your booking today, and several days from now, he will deliver your tickets and the *Credentials* and *Letters of Introduction* you will need when you arrive in Yokohama, for processing by the authorities."

"*Processing by the authorities?*" Hamish asked, puzzled.

"Of course, Mr. Boyd. While you will be most welcome in my country, you must realize you will be a stranger, a *foreigner* – and your credentials must be vetted. But do not fret, we shall provide all that you will require. Now, may I present you with pen and paper so you may prepare your list of required supplies?"

Several hours later, Hamish returned to his studio, having visited his former apprentice at the docks and informed him of his imminent departure. The excited young man would gladly begin his orientation in the morning!

He had also stopped at a flea market and purchased another small trunk – to supplement the one he had brought from Santa Rosa nearly a dozen years earlier. In addition, he found several cheap, torn old blankets and quilts to protect his valuable camera during the long, rolling sea voyage. They would shortly be sent to the Irish washerwoman around the corner, for a thorough laundering before they would be packed.

• Adam Anthony •

FOUR

On the morning of his departure for Japan, Hamish was assisted in getting his trunks to the harbor by his former apprentice. Since the latter was anxious to return to the studio for his first solo portrait sitting, their final words were brief. As he left, Hamish felt confident the eager young man would serve him well during his long absence.

Hamish then turned his attention to the clamor and chaos all around him. Wagons and carriages were pulling up, one after another, trunks and supplies were unloaded, and passengers and some apparent members of the ship's staff, were disgorged.

All this was happening alongside a beautiful, apparently quite new, wooden-hulled paddlewheel, coal-fired steamship. When his tickets were delivered to him the previous week, a small pamphlet was included, describing these features. In addition, prospective passengers were also informed that *this* craft was a smaller version of a famous paddlewheel steamship – *The China*, which had been in service for some time between San Francisco and Hong Kong. Hamish was also told that – as in the case of the larger, apparently more-luxurious *China*, he would have access to a long Promenade Deck, for outdoor exercise, and a variety of other activities which would be detailed once the vessel was underway.

The pamphlet further made clear that there were two tiers of accommodations onboard – *Cabin* and *Compartment*, and his tickets indicated he was booked, each way, into the latter. He would soon discover the difference between them.

Presently, two lines of passengers were being formed by crew members, to go onboard in an orderly fashion. Signs on tripods indicated *Cabin* passengers to the right, *Compartment* passengers to the left. All passengers were told their trunks would be delivered to their quarters, shortly.

After Hamish saw his tiny compartment, he wondered if he could tolerate almost four weeks at sea, in such a small enclosure. The door, upon swinging open into the corridor, revealed a mere foot or so of space before one encountered bunk beds, one above the other, against the opposite wall. A petite lamp was mounted on the wall for evening use and a very small glass porthole was located alongside the upper bunk bed – to allow in daylight and moonlight. A covered chamber pot was positioned on the floor beneath the lower bunk bed, leaving minimal room for the storage of luggage. Several clothing hooks were mounted on the limited wall space remaining, and one on the back of the door.

A note placed on the lower bunk directed Compartment-Class passengers to a communal washroom down the corridor. While Hamish awaited the delivery of his trunks, he investigated and found three small sinks with mirrors mounted on the wall above, and a small sitz-bath behind a curtain. A sign on the wall indicated the latter had to be reserved for use with the Corridor Attendant, due to high demand, for an extra fee.

By the time his luggage arrived, Hamish decided to store his small clothing trunk on the floor below the lower bunk, and place the one containing his camera *on* the lower bed itself – cushioned by its mattress, pillow and blankets against jostling by the rolling sea. He would sleep on the upper bunk.

Later, he strode the Promenade Deck while the ship pulled out of San Francisco harbor. The views were magnificent! He so wished he could photograph them, but the lack of collodion and his inability to keep the camera steady at sea – as well as problems maintaining long, immobile exposures as objects passed by, due to the ship's movement, made this impossible. It was then that he decided to keep a sketchbook during the voyage, using some of the writing paper he had brought with him for corresponding with his landlord and the lad who was tending to his studio.

After they were out of sight of the harbor, the Corridor Attendants gathered up the passengers into small groups, based upon their shipboard accommodations, and provided tours of the public areas of the ship. The men were shown a small Gymnasium for their use, the women a Music Room – where needlework and gentile conversation were welcome when concerts and musical entertainments were not being presented.

Both men and women would have regular access to the ship's Library, which appeared to be divided into two sections: *Japanese* books and periodicals and *American* ones. Hamish noticed that issues of *Harper's New Monthly Magazine* and *The Atlantic Monthly* – although dated, were present among the latter.

There would also be periodic demonstrations of *traditional* Japanese arts, mainly for the American passengers, during the voyage. Some of these would occur in the Music Room, some on the Promenade Deck. Hamish and most of the others were confused when quick mention was made of *Kabuki* and

Bunraku performances, although later in the voyage, when he attended them, their mysteries would be revealed. Japanese jugglers would also entertain after dinner most nights – and there would be concerts with ancient Japanese musical instruments, flower-arranging demonstrations, exhibitions of ancient Japanese court dancing, and the intricacies of the formal Japanese tea ceremony. Hamish rightly predicted that he and the other men onboard would likely avoid many of the latter events.

After lunch that first day, in a long narrow galley intersected by an etched-glass screen to separate the two classes of passengers, Hamish attempted to retire to his Compartment for a nap. However, the suffocating feeling of the tiny room made such an endeavor difficult – so he went and sat in a deck chair on the Promenade and began his first sketches.

On the way there, he pretended to be "lost", as he deliberately wandered into the *Cabin* corridor. He quickly glanced into the open door of a vacant chamber and was impressed by the relative size and opulence therein – compared with his own *Compartment*. But then, he was caught out by the Corridor Attendant, who promptly directed the "lost soul" back to the Promenade.

As the voyage proceeded in the days to follow, Hamish came to tire of the endless sea, sky and occasional birds on the horizon, and found himself focusing on the ship's Staff. Several times he caught glimpses of the men who stoked coal in the bowels of the ship, as they surfaced for a bit of fresh sea air while they sat at the entrance to the ship's lowest chambers. They looked very grimy and tired, and they appeared to be perpetually chewing on something that looked like a large biscuit.

One day, he asked his Corridor Attendant what the stokers were eating all the time, and the noticeably-uncomfortable gentleman appeared embarrassed that such denizens of the bowels of the ship had been observed by a passenger. After clearing his throat in a bid to collect his thoughts and consider the implications of his response, he answered Hamish, "It is *sea bread*, Sir."

Hamish pointedly remarked, "I see. It looks to be a mite plain, I reckon even tasteless. Is that *all* they eat?"

The startled and obviously-perturbed Attendant now added, "It is but the *hardtack* soldiers had to eat all through the War between the North and the South, Sir."

Later in the voyage, Hamish would have occasion to remember this conversation. When passing the slightly-open door of the galley kitchen after a meal, he saw several of the kitchen staff quickly devouring the leftover scraps on the dirty plates of the departing passengers – prior to their being washed before the next meal. He could not help but wonder if these apparently-underfed men ever shared their meager bounty with the poor souls laboring below.

By the end of the second week of the voyage, Hamish began to wonder if he would survive the boredom and monotony of this long trip – enlivened mainly by occasional calls at island ports along the way to restock food and fuel. For as much as he tried to amuse himself with sketching, exercising in the Gymnasium, reading in the Library – and the unexpectedly-interesting Kabuki theatrical performances and clever Bunraku puppet shows, he was very lonely. Most of the passengers residing in the Compartments appeared to be American merchants on their way to seek fame and fortune in the mysterious land once known as *Nippon*. And the Cabin-class occupants appeared to be haughty, wealthy tourists, who when encountered on the Promenade and elsewhere were not inclined to directly socialize with any outside their *circle*.

And so, he frequently had reason to fear he would not be coherent by the time he arrived at Yokohama Harbor.

FIVE

As his steamship pulled into Yokohama Harbor Hamish stood on the Promenade Deck, with his trunks beside him, and offered a brief, silent prayer of thanksgiving for his safe passage.

He could hardly wait to disembark and stand on solid land again. Several times during the journey, while making stops at ports-of-call to replenish supplies, the Captain allowed passengers to stretch their legs dockside. And while Hamish enjoyed the physical and emotional relief these moments provided, they only increased his desire for this long journey to end.

Today, as soon as the whistle blew – signaling permission to leave the ship, a cadre of eager porters waiting on the dock rushed onto the vessel, offering their services. Upon seeing his trunks, several approached Hamish and after bowing, pointed to them. Hamish nodded and smiled broadly, in what he assumed was a universal indication of assent, and then headed for the departure ramp while the porters followed.

When they reached the dock, he was prepared to pay the porters with a small amount of Japanese currency Mr. Hasegawa had included in the packet with his tickets. The packet also included a note suggesting that he convert some of his American currency as soon as possible upon arrival. However, the porters remained close to him and the trunks, indicating they were not yet ready to be dismissed. *They* knew what lay ahead for new arrivals.

As Hamish looked around, he relished the strange, colorful sights, as well as the variety of nautical conveyances in the water nearby – including small boats which were rowed with a scull from the stern, some even having a sail or awning. Soon, he would learn they were called *sampan*.

His photographer's eye was recording the colorful imagery, so much more stimulating than the endless sky and sea which dominated his voyage. During that time, he was so desperate to break the monotonous sea-views, that he rejoiced when a small atoll came into view, for a brief period while his ship passed by.

His reverie was soon interrupted, however, when figures in uniforms approached, bowed to the crowd of recently-arrived passengers and directed them – in British-accented English, to come along to have their credentials processed.

At the nearby processing center, alongside the dock, among other matters Hamish was required to declare his intentions in coming to Japan – and where he would be residing. When he showed his credentials from the Japanese Consulate back in San Francisco, and the letter which vouchsafed his pending employment by Prince Kashiwara, the official processing him quickly bowed and waved him toward the currency conversion counter, next to the exit.

Later, as Hamish and the porters left the building, the latter escorted him to the railroad station, where he and most of the other passengers were to take the train to Tokyo. As they walked along, one of the Japanese policemen accompanying them proudly told the group only two years earlier, Emperor Meiji himself had inaugurated this eighteen-mile rail service between Yokohama and Tokyo.

Upon reaching the train, one of the onboard officials greeted Hamish with the customary stiff bow, and asked for his tickets. The official then uttered something in Japanese to the porters who still guarded Hamish's trunks, as if with their lives, and they led the way to his shared compartment. There were metal racks mounted above the seats, large enough for his small trunks. After the porters secured the latter in place, they bowed again and silently stood still. It was then that Hamish realized it was now time to pay them. But how much?

He pulled out his Japanese currency and stared at it. At that moment the Carriage Attendant appeared, bowed and pointed to several *yen* notes in Hamish's hand. The Attendant gingerly removed them and handed them to the porters, indicating the expected amount of payment for the porters' services. Hamish was grateful for the intervention and bowed in return.

Early in his stay, Hamish would learn of the currency chaos which followed the fall of the Tokugawa Shogunate and the Meiji Restoration. As a result, he was told, the new government was impelled to pass the *Currency Act of 1871* – which led to the creation of the yen in 1872. The yen notes, known to the Japanese as *tsuhosatu*, were printed in faraway Germany and were based on the *gold* standard preferred by many of Japan's new international trading partners. However, since Asian nations were still partial to *silver*, the Meiji government also issued silver coins.

For the present, however, during his journey to Tokyo the train moved slowly enough for Hamish to enjoy the passing scene – the architecture, flora, birds, laborers in the fields. He was especially surprised to note that so many Japanese who were walking near the tracks stopped upon seeing the on-coming train and bowed stiffly to the passengers onboard. Many of the latter were leaning out their carriage windows, waving and laughing loudly – perhaps somewhat giddy from their weeks at sea. Hamish noted that the males they passed bowed in the same fashion, hands straight down their sides, as the various Japanese staff he had encountered since leaving San Francisco. The passing women, however, placed their clasped hands across their stomachs while doing so.

When the train eventually arrived at the Tokyo station, a cadre of porters politely escorted the passengers and their luggage off the train and to a nearby area where local transportation could be arranged. In anticipation of this moment, Hamish had received instructions from the Consulate before his departure that one of the Prince's servants would be waiting for him, holding a sign with his name on it. Very quickly, he noticed the individual – a small, thin, elderly gentleman, dressed in a simple Western-style black suit. Hamish approached him and bowed in the Japanese fashion.

The servant then bowed several times in rapid succession, before guiding Hamish and his porters to a small horse-drawn cart, where the porters were instructed to deposit the trunks. Then the servant took Hamish to a nearby *jinrikisha*, and once he was settled in, the servant returned to the porters and paid them, on Hamish's behalf. He then signaled the jinrikisha to follow him.

Hamish couldn't help but notice that the jinrikisha in which he rode for the first time resembled a Western *hansom cab* in some respects – particularly in regard to its retractable hood. Soon, he would learn that the person who pulled these vehicles was known as a *runner*. And not long after that, he would be introduced to the rapid Westernization of Japanese words occurring in Meiji Japan – as he heard American and British visitors refer to such conveyances as *rickshaws*, for example.

When they appeared to have left the commercial area and entered a residential one, Hamish glanced at his pocket watch and determined the journey had taken forty-five minutes. Soon, the Prince's servant drove the small cart through a traditional Japanese wooden gate and into what Hamish correctly assumed had to be the Prince's estate.

Hamish had been expecting a large, palatial complex – after all, his host was *royalty*, but the buildings grouped around the courtyard were rather modest. The wooden entrance gate was bordered by dense vegetation on both sides, across the front of the property, and the other three perimeters of the estate were similarly landscaped with close-set trees and shrubbery.

Hamish assumed the largest building – at the back of the courtyard, was the Prince's private residence. He also recognized an obvious carriage house/stable just to the right, inside the gate. Before the day was out, he would learn that the servant and his wife resided there, in a single room on the upper floor.

When both conveyances stopped in front of a small building – a short distance to the left of the main villa, the Prince's servant spoke in Japanese to the jinrikisha runner, who quickly removed Hamish's trunks from the cart and carried them up the three steps leading to the porch and the building's front door. It was obvious this was the guest house – destined to be Hamish's quarters during his stay. The runner then removed his shoes and carried the trunks inside. While this was occurring, Hamish also noticed a small pavilion directly opposite the guest house, on the far side of the courtyard. Before the evening was over, he would learn this was the Prince's private teahouse.

Once the trunks were inside, the servant paid the runner, and after the latter left, Hamish was directed through the door to his quarters – having been shown to remove his shoes, *first*.

And thus began Hamish's introduction to a *very* different world.

SIX

After the Prince's servant left him alone, Hamish realized that despite the Japanese emphasis on manners and courtesy – which he had witnessed among fellow Japanese travelers and staff onboard ship, and in his encounters with everyone he met in Japan so far, the servant *never* introduced himself. He referred to Hamish as *Mr. Boyd* since they met at the train station, but said little else to him afterward. In fact, the longest conversation they had was that which occurred when he showed Hamish his sleeping quarters and washroom at the guesthouse – before informing him of the hour he would return to escort him to dinner at the Prince's villa.

When Hamish explored the small space where he would reside for some months, he noted it was larger than the simple living area behind his studio, but not much more so. The exterior walls of the guesthouse were very thin, he reckoned, and he wondered how the Japanese were able to stay warm in cold weather. This thought made him much relieved to realize he would be returning home just as autumn began to appear later in the year.

The interior walls were unfamiliar – wooden latticework in various patterns, with paper stretched over it. By the next morning, he would learn from the Prince's servant, upon asking, that such walls were called *shoji*. And he also discovered, within the building's interior, folding screens which appeared to be used to define functional spaces. He would later be told these screens, decorated with a variety of painted designs, were called *byobu*.

The sleeping area was located behind a large six-panel screen – and was dominated by a rather thin pallet lying on the tatami-mat covered floor. Nearby were several low, small storage chests for his meager personal belongings. Another screen separated the washroom area, and another a space where the servant had told him he could store his camera and related equipment until he talked with the Prince – presumably about his working arrangements.

Hamish glanced at his pocket watch and realized it would be several hours until dinner, and in view of his traveler's fatigue, decided it would be best for him to take a nap in the meantime. He settled onto the somewhat uncomfortable floor pallet and soon fell fast asleep, from exhaustion.

It was the soft voice of the Prince's servant which aroused him some time later, and as he rose from the floor with such stiff muscles that he wondered if he could endure four months of such nightly discomfort, he was led to the washroom where the servant had prepared a bowl of hot water and a towel, for him to refresh himself.

As the servant later led him up the front steps to the villa's entrance door, Hamish was filled with anticipation. He had never met *royalty* before!

Once inside the front door, after removing his shoes, Hamish was a bit disoriented. For one, the building appeared to be very sparsely furnished – and in no way *palatial*. Also, what furniture he could see, as he was led to the waiting Prince, was *Western-style*, and not like the traditional furnishings of the guesthouse.

As he was ushered into the Prince's presence, the

latter was found sitting in a large carved chair at the head of a dining table. Hamish had all he could do to control his surprise, his shock. Instead of a regal figure of impressive bearing, the gentleman seated before him was small in stature, dressed in a plain black Western-style suit, and wore small spectacles – held together by the thinnest of silver wire frames. Hamish decided he might as well be meeting a loan officer in a bank back home!

Hamish composed himself quickly and started to make the customary Japanese bow, but his host rose and extended his right hand to shake. This caused Hamish to stop in mid-bow, uncertain as to how to proceed. The Prince came to his rescue.

"We observe the Western customs in my home and at the workshop," he uttered with a smile, and then he and Hamish completed the gesture of a gentlemanly Western greeting.

Now at ease, and a bit less confused, Hamish waited for further direction and the Prince quickly waved him into a chair opposite his own at the table. After he was seated, the Prince continued.

"Yes, I believe in the modern approach to living – my home is therefore furnished throughout in the Western style of this room."

This remark encouraged Hamish to slowly look around without appearing overly intrusive, and it was obvious that except for a few Japanese *objets d'art*, the dining room was outfitted in the style of a proud, prosperous merchant's home back in San Francisco. He had been in a number of such domiciles because wealthy clients often preferred to be photographed amidst their personal treasures, rather than in a studio setting.

And then, as if he could read Hamish's mind, the Prince added, "Ah, yes – the *ryokan!*"

Hamish looked up, confused. "Begging your pardon, Sir. What did you say?"

"The ryokan – the guesthouse where you are lodging. You must be wondering why it is furnished in our traditional style, in view of what I previously said. I am unfortunately impelled to keep it that way due to very occasional visits from the Dowager Princess, my mother. She resides in Kyoto with my married sister, and rarely comes to stay here in Tokyo – she finds this city too *modern,* but when she does, she refuses to live in the Western style. In fact, I regret to say, she does not socially accept *gaijin* – foreigners, being of the old school.

"I see," Hamish responded, silently cursing the Dowager Princess for being responsible for his uncomfortable pallet, while the Prince likely enjoyed a comfortable modern bed. And then, before he could inquire if the lady-in-question would be visiting soon, the perceptive Prince interjected.

"She is aware I have a business associate here from America for a long visit until autumn, and will not be coming before then."

Hamish smiled in relief, for he would rather be housed in this residential setting than in a Japanese inn in the commercial district of Tokyo, most likely surrounded by individuals not very proficient in English. This thought led him to raise the issue of the *English* language with the Prince.

"Begging your pardon, Sir, but you speak mighty fine English. When did you learn? Even your servant knew enough English words so him and me had no trouble talking together today."

"Ah, yes, Mr. Boyd. Some of us in Japan, from

the better-educated classes, started to take English lessons from British tutors as soon as the Tokugawa Shogunate collapsed. We knew which way the wind would blow in the future. And I have taught a bit to Mr. Saigo and his wife, as I have occasional business guests here from abroad."

"Mr. and Mrs. Saigo – they are your servants? I did not know their names."

"That is my fault, Mr. Boyd, as I told them it was my responsibility to introduce you. For their part, they have been instructed to address you as *Mr. Boyd* and I would suggest you call them *Mr. and Mrs. Saigo*. For myself, I would prefer *Purinsu Kashiwara,* or *Purinsu*. That title is a Western corruption of the traditional Japanese word for *Prince*, but I find it easy for my Western colleagues to remember and pronounce. And now, formalities over, let us eat."

The Prince then struck a small bronze gong at his side, with an equally small bronze hammer, and the elderly servants appeared, bearing china plates and Western-style forks and knives.

"This is Mr. and Mrs. Saigo, Mr. Boyd. They have been with me many years. They will tend to you when I am not in need of them myself. Mrs. Saigo will prepare meals which she will deliver to the ryokan when you are in residence, and tend to your housekeeping, laundry and bed linen. Mr. Saigo will tend to your more personal needs, your *valet* to some extent, in areas where it would be inappropriate for his wife to do so. They live in the carriage house, so they are always at one's beck-and-call. In fact, Mr. Saigo will take us to the workshop each day in my best carriage. Since Mr. Saigo knows somewhat more English than his wife, sometimes your instructions to her may have to be relayed through *him*."

• The Meiji Prince •

At this point the Prince nodded to the Saigos, who quickly brought forth the food to be eaten on the china plates and with Western cutlery. Hamish was relieved at the absence of *chopsticks*. During one of the orientation sessions on the ship, to acquaint passengers with Japanese customs, he had failed to master them, and feared being unable to eat comfortably once he arrived in Japan.

After dinner, once the table had been cleared, the Prince lit up a large cigar and offered one to Hamish, who politely declined. While he enjoyed a bit of liquor now and then, he had never taken to tobacco. And just as this thought crossed his mind, Mr. Saigo entered the room with two *sake* cups and a small decanter.

As the Prince poured, he asked, "Are you familiar with our native wine, made from fermented rice, Mr. Boyd? It is called sake."

"Yes, Purinsu – it was served onboard ship several times while coming over. It is mighty powerful!"

The Prince laughed, and then turned to business.

"Tomorrow I shall take you to my workshop in the commercial district of the City. The photographic supplies you ordered back in San Francisco have arrived from the distributor in Yokohama, so you may begin to instruct my staff promptly. But first, of course, I shall orient you to the woodcut print souvenir postcards which I currently produce and sell and hope to largely replace with photographic ones, now you are here. One must keep up with the times!"

Hamish nodded, feeling very drowsy after several cups of sake.

"In order to make it easier for you to have a convenient studio and darkroom here at the villa, I shall authorize you to direct Mr. Saigo in the temporary conversion of the *chashitsu*, for that purpose."

Even in his drowsy state, Hamish recognized an unfamiliar Japanese word, and his confusion was apparently written all over his face.

"I beg your pardon, Mr. Boyd, the teahouse opposite the guesthouse – the chashitsu. And you may set up your camera there also, as I have ordered several new ones for you to train my staff on at the workshop – therefore your studio here will be totally independent, although I expect you to take photographs there which we can transfer to postcards, of course."

Later in the evening, as Hamish fell asleep on the uncomfortable floor pallet, he could only imagine what the Prince's Western-style bed might look like – and feel like. He also continued to fail to reconcile the expectations he had for his royal employer's appearance and demeanor, with that of the reality of the man-in-the-flesh.

SEVEN

The next morning, Mr. Saigo drove Hamish and the Prince to the latter's workshop in the commercial district of Tokyo. They rode in a black Hansom-cab-style carriage for two, while Mr. Saigo stood behind the passenger compartment and guided the horse. Hamish would later learn it was the Prince's *best* carriage.

When they arrived in front of the building the Prince owned, and alighted, he instructed Mr. Saigo to return at the usual time at the end of the workday. He and Hamish then proceeded toward the front door of the building.

Hamish instinctively began to remove his shoes on the small porch – puzzled that there were not already a number of items of footwear stacked there (*Surely,* he thought, *the staff has already arrived!*) However, the Prince stopped him from so doing.

"Ah, Mr. Boyd – how quickly you learn our traditional customs. However, that is only required when walking on wooden floors or tatami mats. Since I have so many foreign visitors coming here for souvenirs to take home, I designed this building with *stone* floors. You need only wipe the soles of your shoes on the thick straw mat in front of the door, and enter."

This unexpected turn of events pleased Hamish, as he had been concerned about the prospect of working in stocking feet, while handling chemicals which occasionally splashed or spilled onto his arms, feet or the floor.

The front door opened directly into the Postcard Shop where customers, both foreign and domestic, purchased the woodblock-print souvenir postcards the Prince and his staff had been producing for several years. A small display window facing the street – much like that next to the entrance of Hamish's studio back in San Francisco, contained examples of the wares available for sale.

Once inside the Shop, the Prince showed Hamish a sampling of the merchandise currently for sale. The postcards were of the standard Western-size, as far as Hamish could ascertain, and appeared to fall into two categories: those depicting traditional scenes and those which illustrated the many modern changes occurring in Meiji Japan. Prince Kashiwara quickly elaborated.

"Many travelers like to purchase contrasting pairs to take home. Here, let me show you an example."

He then took two cards and placed them on the narrow counter, before Hamish.

"You see, the one on the left depicts a traditional Japanese house, but the one on the right is clearly a Western-style home – *Victorian Meiji*, as we call the style here. It would likely be that of a newly-wealthy merchant who has capitalized on the opening of Japan to Western trading nations. When we expand our inventory with the addition of *photographic* versions of these woodblock-print postcards – now you are here, I shall be expecting you to provide views showing similar contrasts between the old and the new."

"I see," Hamish responded, more entranced by the traditional architectural images on display than the ones which resembled buildings one might find in San Francisco. Then he added, "I see many are colored, not just black and white."

"Oh, yes – those are more expensive of course, since coloring a woodblock print is a tedious process, involving much additional labor and time. But foreign customers generally prefer the colored ones. Let me now take you to the Engraving Room," he added, as he led Hamish through a door to the right of the Postcard Shop. As they passed into that area it registered with Hamish that the interior walls in the building had been constructed Western-style; there were no shoji screens about.

In the Engraving Room, Hamish was introduced to the engravers and artists who, like every other employee he was to meet that day, were male, dressed in simple Western-style work clothes and spoke limited, but passable, English.

He was told that an artist first completed a drawing, which a copyist then traced onto a sheet of translucent paper. Afterward, the engraver pasted the copy, face down, on a hard cherry-wood block and cut away parts of the block – leaving the lines to be printed in relief. These blocks, with their relief lines, were then taken to the Print Shop where black ink was applied. This block was known as the *key block*.

Once in the Print Shop, the printers showed him the tedious process whereby *each* color that would appear in the final print had to be added to the key block, separately. He was told that the recent replacement of watercolors, with imported aniline dyes, created the more vivid colors foreign tourists favored, and also made the multi-stage process much easier.

By the time Hamish watched the various stages which transformed a woodblock engraving into a printed postcard for sale in the Postcard Shop, he could not help remarking, "Making photographic postcards will be mighty faster and easier, Purinsu!"

"Which is precisely *why* you are here, Mr. Boyd," his employer answered, with alacrity. He then turned the conversation to *photography*.

"I believe you have seen enough to understand our current operation. Let me now show you your Studio and Darkroom. They are on the other side of the Postcard Shop."

Hamish was then led to the new Studio. The room was large, with but one window on the far wall. It was bordered by heavy Western-style window drapes and thin under-curtains on a rod, allowing one to shut out or admit light as desired. Several new cameras were in place, on tripods. Hamish rushed over to examine them. They were clearly of the best quality currently available for use with the tedious wet collodion process. For a moment he struggled not to verbalize what was on his mind – *Why isn't the dry plate process available yet? It will be so much easier*! But his reverie was broken by the Prince's voice.

"And now let me show you the Darkroom, where the supplies you requested have been stored since their arrival from Yokohama."

The Darkroom had a small, narrow, horizontal high window, whose light could be minutely adjusted by a tiny sliding shoji screen. Hamish would have to experiment to achieve the proper illumination while developing images on the glass plates. A table was set up along the opposite wall, waiting for Hamish to arrange the metal pans and solutions he would need during the developing process. As he inspected the crates which were stacked nearby, a thought occurred to him.

"It would be a mite easier if I had me a few shelves in here to store all these bottles, the glass plates and the rest," he said to the Prince.

"Of course, Mr. Boyd. It shall be done as soon as possible. Let us go to my Office and prepare the order for one of my assistants to take to a vendor who provides such merchandise and is located nearby."

The Prince's Office was behind the Postcard Shop and was furnished in the Western style, with a large desk, several chairs, and wooden file cabinets. He sat behind the desk and beckoned Hamish to sit in one of the chairs opposite. He then asked Hamish to sketch the shelving he needed, including dimensions. When Hamish was done, the Prince examined the sketch and annotated it with Japanese characters, before going to the doorway and summoning one of the Card Shop staff. After showing the sketch to the obviously-eager young man, and saying a few words in Japanese, the Prince turned to Hamish.

"I would suggest, Mr. Boyd, you join this gentleman on his trip to the local cabinet-maker down the street."

As Hamish and the other man were leaving, the Prince added, "If we finish arranging the Darkroom by day's end, I shall let you spend tomorrow setting up your Studio and Darkroom at the teahouse back at my villa. In fact, if you will also need shelving and a table there – as I assume you must, you may order a duplicate set from this merchant today. My assistant will do the translation for you – the cabinet-maker does not speak English, I regret to say. And if he has what you need in stock, tell him to deliver it to you at the villa tomorrow, while the rest should come here today."

With that, Hamish and the assistant rushed to

the door. At last, after so little activity onboard ship, for so long, Hamish was now again ready to *create beautiful images*. This, he realized – now more than ever before, was his life's blood.

EIGHT

By the time Hamish crossed the villa's courtyard the next morning, to set up his studio in the Prince's teahouse, he was in high spirits.

The previous day, the cabinet-maker to whom the Prince had sent him and an assistant, was obviously overjoyed when he learned of the Prince's patronage. He quickly studied the sketch they had brought and led them to his warehouse stockroom. While not identical to the shelving Hamish had sketched, the ready-made items were sufficiently appropriate for his purposes – as was a table that was also in stock. And luckily, there were enough of these items for both the workshop Studio and that at the villa.

An hour later, the table and shelves for the workshop were delivered and Hamish spent the rest of the day arranging the photographic equipment and supplies the Prince had ordered during his long journey to Japan. When he was done, he showed the Studio and Darkroom to the Prince.

"Very impressive, Mr. Boyd," the Prince remarked, as he inspected the area. "But I wonder if the Studio is too bare. All I see are cameras on tripods. Do you not need some furnishings to add interest to the photographs you will be taking here?"

Hamish glanced around the room and immediately realized it clearly lacked the features of his establishment back in San Francisco. There, he had some vases, small bits of furniture, a statuary bust and silk flowers – but nothing like that was *here*.

"Of course, Purinsu – I plumb forgot about them!"

The Prince smiled, in self-satisfaction. He wanted to keep a bit of an upper-hand with Hamish – after all, he was but a humble employee. But he preferred to do so in a non-confrontational manner, such as this.

"Do not worry, Mr. Boyd. We are just beginning our adventure here. While you are at my villa tomorrow, I shall visit the local market and purchase a few small, typically-Japanese items. Since there appears to be some vacant space on the shelves in the Darkroom, we can store some of them there. Any others can be stored behind a folding screen which I shall also purchase as a backdrop for the Studio. I assume we will eventually need *several* such screens, to vary the background of the photographs, shall we not?"

"That's a fine idea, Purinsu," Hamish replied, relieved to know that the Prince obviously had an aesthetic sensibility, even if he had not yet learned the intricacies of photography.

Hamish's recollections of the previous day's events were interrupted by the return of Mr. Saigo, from having taken the Prince to the workshop this morning. He drove the carriage up to the front of the teahouse, and as he climbed down, motioned to Hamish – who noticed he'd brought with him some of the Darkroom supplies from the workshop. Hamish nodded in appreciation, and then they carefully carried them into the teahouse.

While Hamish set up his camera on its tripod, Mr. Saigo left to stable the horse. When he returned, he found Hamish examining items he found in the room, which were obviously used in conducting the tea ceremony – bowls, a scoop, hot pads, cups, tea caddies, a small storage cabinet. There was also a delicately-painted folding screen in the room. It occurred to Hamish that any of these items might be of use when taking photographs, and the folding screen could be used as a backdrop, as well as a place behind which to store such items when they were not needed.

Mr. Saigo then showed him a small, dark storage area which had a very high, narrow, horizontal window, making it perfect for use as a darkroom – almost a duplicate of that back at the workshop. This was where he would put the shelving and the table, expected later in the day.

Shortly after lunch, the cabinet-maker's son drove his father's wagon into the courtyard, after which he and Mr. Saigo carried the shelving and the table into the teahouse. Hamish supervised their placement, and after they left to attend to other duties, he stocked the shelves and arranged the table for the plate-coating, plate-sensitizing and plate-developing processes.

By the time Mr. Saigo brought the Prince home at the end of the workday, the latter was very impressed with Hamish's accomplishments so far.

"This teahouse will make a fine studio for you Mr. Boyd. I believe this is where we should arrange portrait sittings for the higher-class residents of Tokyo – the wealthy merchants, members of the military – perhaps even of the Royal Family, although to date, my relatives only allow themselves to be photographed at the Imperial Palace and Gardens. But who knows? At any rate, those are not personages we would want to come in their finery and uniforms to the commercial district where the workshop is located. *That* location is fine for those of less distinction. In the future, I shall review the requests for portraits and direct the customers according to status, either to your studio here, or the one at the workshop."

"Whatever you wish, Purinsu." Hamish responded. By this early stage in his employment by the Prince, he had already consciously decided to do whatever he was told during the next four months, before his return journey homeward. The salary he was being paid was too generous, and the opportunity to be in Japan too rare, to jeopardize them by not being obsequious, when necessary.

"Also," the Prince continued, "for any portrait sittings you arrange on your own, through contacts you may make while here, you may keep twenty-five percent of the profit – in addition to your salary."

Hamish visibly blushed a deep scarlet, and responded, "I reckon that is plenty generous, Purinsu. Thank you."

The Prince was momentarily startled by the visible deep blush on Hamish's pale face – so well suited to the overall appearance created by his full head of blond hair and blond mustache. He made a mental note to watch for it during future encounters. It could be a sign of his employee's true feelings on matters too delicate for him to discuss openly. And then, he spoke once more.

"I believe the past two days have been very productive – an excellent start for our new adventure. Therefore, I would like to invite you to dine with me tonight at the villa. Mr. or Mrs. Saigo will fetch you at the appointed time."

And with that, he turned and left the teahouse.

NINE

When Hamish returned to the workshop the following day, he found several small decorative items in the Studio. The Prince told him he had purchased them the day before, to add interest to photographs taken there in the future.

Hamish examined them and noted they included painted Japanese hand fans, vases filled with silk flowers, and several folding screens. It occurred to him that he lacked a tall plinth of the type against which gentlemen often posed in photographs of the period. He mentioned this to the Prince.

"Of course, Mr. Boyd – it would especially be useful for portraits of married couples, where the husband would be resting his elbow on the plinth and his wife seated nearby. I have seen that pose in Western photographs before. I shall order *two*, as you will need one at the teahouse, also. But I believe that *now* we need to start acquainting my staff with these new cameras."

Hamish went over to the cameras, which were lined up side-by-side, and waited for the Prince to bring several of his much-valued and brightest assistants into the Studio. Soon he returned with three young men.

"These are very faithful workers, who are most

interested in becoming photographers," he told Hamish.

The assistants extended their hands in a Western-style greeting, and Hamish reciprocated. Then he began the first lesson, having decided to use one of the cameras for the students to manipulate and practice upon, while he used the other for instructional purposes.

Recalling the manner in which he was trained during his own apprenticeship years earlier, he began at the most basic level – describing and locating the parts of the camera and the tripod upon which it rested.

Hamish spent several days making sure that his students were completely familiar with the camera, its operation, and parts – including the shutter, the squeeze bulb which opened the shutter, the *back hole* through which one looked to be sure the scene was ready for exposing the plate, and the black cloth which served to cover the camera and keep extraneous light away from the plate.

During this time, he also showed them – using unprepared glass plates, how one put the plate in a wooden frame which one then slid into the camera before exposure, to be removed afterwards for developing while the plate was still wet. He stressed that the plate had to remain motionless during exposure – by mounting the camera securely on the tripod, rather than holding the camera in one's hand. He told them it was also advantageous, if one had an assistant, to have that individual hold the plate in place to avoid even slight movements. Otherwise, a lone photographer had to both monitor the exposure time *and* hold the plate in place.

After several days of exercises on the camera itself, Hamish felt satisfied his students were ready

• The Meiji Prince •

to advance to the wet collodion plate process – all the way through to final development and printing. Therefore, he showed them how to prepare the glass plate: to coat it with collodion, and then sensitize it with silver salts. He used that plate to take a photograph of the three of them, afterward showing them how to develop it and print it. They were delighted with the results. When those tasks had been mastered, under his close supervision, he started taking regular photographs in the Studio.

The subjects he initially photographed, largely for instructional purposes, were close at hand. One was the Prince, who was delighted to have his portrait taken, while posing in several different changes of clothing – sometimes wearing a hat or holding a cigar. The Prince chose one of these poses for reproduction as a carte-de-visite, for social and business purposes. One of the cartes, as well as one of his larger portraits, was put on display in the Card Shop window, in an attempt to attract customers.

Hamish's students delighted in being photographed, and soon participated in exotic scenarios which were presented in frozen tableaux style – wearing elaborate traditional Japanese costumes provided by the Prince. These poses of Japanese men in costume generated postcards popular with tourists, when displayed in the Card Shop window. Even more popular were photographs of young women in beautiful kimonos – models hired by the Prince and dressed in costly garments which, he confided to Hamish, had to be *rented* from local theatrical companies due to their prohibitive cost.

Soon, postcards followed which depicted the tea ceremony, flower arranging, as well as Japanese persons in modern Western dress – to emphasize the desire of the Meiji Restoration to modernize Japan. The Prince became very involved in the photographic operation and several times even arranged for a small jinrikisha to be brought into the studio where he posed a *runner* at the front and a *passenger* sitting in the conveyance waiting to be taken to his or her destination.

The weeks of instruction passed quickly, while Hamish was anxious to start taking photographs in his studio at the villa. Therefore, the Prince ultimately agreed to let him spend two days each week there – Mondays and Tuesdays, and the other three weekdays at the workshop directing the photography and supervising the production of the souvenir postcards. During this time, the Prince arranged several portrait sittings for Hamish to execute, of individuals he did not deem *worthy* of sending to the villa studio. The Prince also graciously decided Hamish should have his weekends free to explore Tokyo, selecting locations for taking outdoor photographs which would lend themselves to postcard reproduction.

The first photograph Hamish took at the villa was of Mr. and Mrs. Saigo, in a formal couple's pose – with him resting his elbow on a four-foot high plinth and she seated stiffly in a nearby chair. Hamish also photographed her arranging flowers and preparing tea in the traditional Japanese way. The Prince approved of these and other photographs he subsequently took at the villa studio, believing they would appeal to tourists.

However, before long the Prince became anxious for Hamish to start photographing *outdoor* scenes – both traditional and modern settings, around the city of Tokyo. Hamish's first attempts failed because he could not get the wet plates back to the darkrooms at the workshop or the villa before they dried.

Hamish explained the problem to the Prince and told him that in the Crimean War, and the more-recent War Between the States, photographers solved this problem by turning wagons or vans into on-site darkrooms. When they were going to be in one place for some time, they often erected a *darkroom tent* for such a purpose. Upon hearing this, the Prince arranged to have the small horse-drawn cart Mr. Saigo used to transport Hamish's trunks from the railroad station to the villa upon his arrival, converted for such a purpose. Hamish directed the construction of a wooden frame over the bed of the cart, which was then covered with the heaviest, light-blocking canvas which could be located.

Soon, Hamish and his traveling darkroom became a *fixture* and *curiosity* when spotted near the ancient gardens, temples, expanding harbor, as well as the modern buildings and construction sites of Tokyo. The Prince was delighted with the photographic results, and soon new postcards replaced those in the Card Shop window – all proving to be popular with the buying public, especially the foreign tourists, temporary foreign embassy staff, and mercantile traders from abroad.

The demand for portraits also grew, and as he had indicated earlier, the Prince continued to determine who would be photographed at the workshop and who at the villa. The best examples of that output were also put on display in the Card Shop window.

Soon, Hamish fell into the pattern of working at the villa on Mondays and Tuesdays, supervising photography and postcard production at the workshop Wednesdays, Thursdays and Fridays – and being free on weekends to work or continue to acquaint himself with this ancient, fascinating city and its residents.

For his part, as the new merchandise was produced and proven to be popular with customers, the Prince was well-pleased with the investment he had made in employing Hamish.

TEN

As time passed, Hamish found himself ill-at-ease with the quality of some of the photographs the Prince's staff were producing when he was away from the workshop. They appeared to him to be rather pedestrian – lacking in aesthetic value. Finally, one day he told the Prince he felt the photographers needed to have their skills *refreshed*, and requested several days for that purpose.

The Prince was nonplussed by Hamish's concerns – stating that he was well-satisfied with the product being generated. He made an attempt to pacify Hamish by agreeing that *his* photographs were of higher quality – and therefore warranted higher prices. But as far as he was concerned, those taken by the assistants were selling well enough, especially among undiscerning tourists. But when it became evident that Hamish was not placated by his response, he agreed to allow him to devote a *single* day for review, in order to put his mind at rest.

The day of the review was very frustrating for Hamish. His three photographic assistants were affable – as usual, but appeared bored and distracted during his review of the processes and procedures involved. No matter how much Hamish tried to ignite their interest in composition, lighting, and other aesthetic elements of *beautiful* photographs, they did not seem enthusiastic. In addition, he sensed they were extremely *tired*. At times, it even appeared they could barely keep their eyes open.

At the end of the day, he noted also the developing and printing supplies were dwindling faster than he had expected, but when he expressed concern to the Prince, the latter told him he now had a standing weekly order with the distributor in Yokohama. This led Hamish to decide the men *were* being driven very hard by the demands of the Prince, on the days when he – a more lenient taskmaster, was not present at the workshop.

The next morning, Hamish requested to see the products ready for shipping to major cities in Japan and abroad. Many of the photographs had the mediocre quality that compelled him to approach the Prince for a review session, on the previous day. However, there were so many cartons packed, sealed and ready for shipping that once again, he determined these young men must be under considerable pressure from their employer, the Prince. And he found himself grateful that the Prince continued to give him, personally, much latitude and freedom in his own work.

At the same time, he was also disappointed to see the quality of the postcard *albums* the workshop was producing. Whether filled with the new photographic images or the traditional woodblock print images, they were clearly cheaply put together. Thin pasteboard covers at the front and back adorned them in a simple fashion, and a label on the front cover indicated, *Views of Tokyo*, or *The Japanese Home*, and the like. Ordinarily, he would not have focused on the quality of the albums, if it had not been for a recent journey he made to photograph the

• The Meiji Prince •

newly-reconstructed *Ginza* shopping and commercial district of Tokyo.

It was the Prince himself who told him one day of the Ginza, a district of Tokyo named after a silver-coin mint established there in 1612, during the Edo Period. Just two years prior to Hamish's arrival in Japan, many of the old wooden buildings in the Ginza had burned to the ground. The new Meiji government seized upon this opportunity to rebuild the area as a major shopping and commercial district – but this time, constructing two-and-three-story *brick* buildings in the Western Georgian style.

So steadfast was the government in this task, the Prince related to Hamish, that in just one year, the first Western-style promenade was completed – from the Shinbashi Bridge to the Kyobashi Bridge. It was there that the Prince directed Hamish to travel with his little darkroom cart, to provide more photographic evidence of the very modern nation of Japan being created under the Meiji.

Hamish subsequently spent several days in the area, taking the kind of photographs the Prince desired of *modern* Japan, but he also took time to examine some of the merchandise in the luxury shops which had moved into the now-high-rent area.

It was in one of those shops, whose beautiful lacquer ware in the street-level display window caught his eye, that he became familiar with this ancient craft. It was an apparently-slow business day, and the clerk who politely attended to him evidently assumed he was a wealthy foreigner – leading him to spend considerable time orienting Hamish to the origin and process behind lacquer ware.

The gentleman explained, in passable English, that *lacquer* is the refined sap of the *lacquer tree*, and was originally applied to wooden containers for a very practical purpose – to waterproof them. It was only later, after the introduction of Buddhism into Japan in the middle of the Sixth Century that the aesthetic possibilities of the process were realized. This initially came about through the production of beautiful lacquer ware objects for religious purposes, but the creative process was soon transferred to expensive secular objects as well.

The clerk further explained that the process of achieving the type of spectacular lacquer ware on display in his establishment was arduous, and consisted of many steps – including the application of multiple layers of lacquer, gold and silver powders, mother-of-pearl and abalone shell inlays, engraving in low relief, and much more. Black and red were the predominant colors for centuries, but the clerk told Hamish that brown, yellow and green were recently being applied due to requests from the buying public – now that demand had spread beyond that traditionally coming from the nobility and Buddhist monks.

During his orientation to these beautiful wares, Hamish focused upon the souvenir woodblock print albums on display, with their lacquered covers of solid wood or wood applied to costly brocade and silk. These covers were works-of-art, as much as the engraved woodblock prints inside. When he learned the price of even the smallest albums, he quickly excused himself – begging an important appointment after glancing at his pocket watch. Upon leaving, he implied he would return soon, but never did.

Now, as he took an objective, jaundiced look at the Prince's albums, he could clearly see their inferiority. The puzzlement for him, however, was that the Prince seemed not to mind. And so, Hamish decided to say nothing further on the matter to the Prince – nor to his photographic assistants.

At the end of the day, he knocked on the door of the Prince's Office, as was his custom – to wait there until Mr. Saigo called with the carriage, to take them both back to the villa. However this time, the Prince apparently rushed to the door – rather than call out, "Enter!" – and held the door half-closed while he told Hamish he would be late, due to evening business in town. He suggested Hamish hire a jinrikisha to take him to the villa.

Hamish nodded, and said, "Good night, Purinsu," – but not before catching a glimpse of a tall, thin, gray-haired Caucasian man wearing spectacles not unlike those of the Prince. The man was leaning over the Prince's desk and from Hamish's vantage point, he was aware the stranger was examining photographs spread across the desk top – but he was too far away to discern their subject matter. He could not be certain if the Prince were displaying photographs *he* had taken or those of his assistants.

As he was leaving the workshop moments later, to hire a jinrikisha runner in the street, he stopped to wish a rather-talkative clerk in the Card Shop a "pleasant evening". Quite impetuously, he asked the young man who the stranger was in the Prince's Office.

"Oh," the young man replied offhandedly, "That is *The Belgian*."

"The Belgian?" Hamish responded.

"Yes, Sir. He is the European distributor of our merchandise. He comes to Japan once each year to view our newest products and arrange for their shipment. I overheard him and the Prince talking about how much sales have risen locally, now you have trained our staff in photography. The Belgian expects sales will now increase in Europe, also."

As Hamish left the young man, he was pleased to know that the considerable investment the Prince had made in a distant stranger from America was proving fruitful for his purposes.

ELEVEN

Prince Kashiwara sat behind his large desk, confident he would not be disturbed. Before locking the door, he had ordered the Card Shop staff to forbid anyone disturbing him, except for one reason: in the event an Imperial messenger arrived, bearing news that the Emperor had accepted his beautifully-prepared invitation for complimentary photographs of His Imperial Highness, the Royal Family and esteemed members of the Court. Kashiwara knew that to receive such a commission would bring incalculable good will and publicity to his firm. And so, he gladly offered the Palace the services of his American photographer, several weeks earlier. Now, in assured privacy, he reviewed the order placed by his European distributor, and tallied the profit he had acquired as a result.

When he accompanied his business partner to the harbor earlier that morning, for his return voyage to Europe on one of the many Dutch trading vessels familiar in Japanese waters long before Commodore Perry arrived, both were in high spirits. They exuded confidence that the new merchandise would sell well – and quickly.

In order to avoid delays in shipping subsequent cartons to Europe, the Prince not only sold the gentleman from Brussels as many completed postcards as he could produce in such a short time, at the usual wholesale price – but also fully-developed glass plates. The latter fetched the Prince upfront premium prices, as he was foregoing royalties on future printings in Brussels. Prince Kashiwara needed cash *now*, because Hamish's arrival had resulted in subsequent new expenses at the workshop.

After he was satisfied that the current sale, and those to come in the future, were going to increase his wealth at a time when such was required, he put away his ledger. But as he was about to unlock the door and announce his availability to his staff, he hesitated, and sat back in his chair.

He was reminded that there remained a particularly-unsettling issue, frequently in his thoughts as of late. Mr. Hamish Boyd had expressed his disappointment with the quality of many of the new items. And, the Prince had to privately admit that they were rushed into production to accommodate the schedule of the visiting gentleman from Belgium. While Hamish no longer discussed the issue openly, the Prince could see the disappointment in his eyes as he reviewed many of the photographs taken by his assistants.

The Prince had come to realize that Hamish's days alone, at the villa or traveling around Tokyo to produce the clearly-superior images which he captured, were likely sustaining him during the remaining months of his contract. As a result, the two had settled into a period of détente, recognizing that the employee's concern with *quality* did not coincide with his employer's concern with *quantity* and profit.

And yet, the Prince was still desirous of finding a way to raise the spirits of this individual who had traveled so far to assist him, and had done so – very conscientiously. *There must be a way to raise his spirits,*

• The Meiji Prince •

the Prince mused. *After all, he will be here several more months.*

And then, it occurred to him! He quickly sent off a messenger to another part of Tokyo, and when the latter returned with a satisfactory response to his query, he asked for Hamish to be summoned to his Office.

Hamish was in the midst of developing some glass plates, and turned the task over to one of his assistants. He then headed to the Office.

"Ah, Mr. Boyd," the Prince exclaimed cheerfully, as Hamish strode up to his desk. "Please close the door and sit down," he added.

After Hamish was settled, the Prince continued. "I have been trying to think of a way to thank you for your extraordinary service to the firm and to me. And I believe I know how that can be done – by providing you with a special Japanese delight."

Hamish leaned forward in his chair and waited for the Prince to continue.

"Have you heard of *geisha* – the special women of Japan?"

Hamish was momentarily taken aback – not having expected such a subject to cross the lips of the Prince. *Of course he had heard of geisha!* During his boring weeks at sea, they were a frequent topic of conversation among the men as they exercised in the ship's small gymnasium. Those conversations were likely fantasy, as most of the persons praising the mythic wonders of the geisha had never met one. And of the several passengers who had, during previous trips to Japan, there was considerable reticence when it came to providing details. They only offered tantalizing hints about the comportment of these fabled mistresses of the art of love.

After a few moments, Hamish composed himself and responded. "Yes, Purinsu, I have heard of them – but have had no doings with them."

"Well, that will soon end, Mr. Boyd. Tonight after dinner one shall arrive at the guesthouse, for your pleasure. I desire to show my gratitude for your service to me and this enterprise."

Hamish did not know what to say in return. He had heard such services were very expensive, and had put aside the thought of any such pleasure while in Japan. He thus practiced – and expected to continue to practice, self-pleasure while in this exotic land.

"I don't reckon I know what to say, Purinsu. I never did expect such a *bonus* in all my born days!"

"Well, it is my pleasure to reward you, Mr. Boyd. I am well-pleased with the excellent instruction you gave my staff. I never expected this new venture to go into full operation so quickly. But you have trained them so well, that we are proceeding ahead of schedule. And the independent work you are producing for me is first quality. So, it is settled then – tonight after dinner."

Later, shortly after Hamish and the Prince arrived back at the villa, with Mr. Saigo driving the carriage, Mrs. Saigo came to the guesthouse with an earlier-than-usual dinner. Hamish noted that in addition to the change in time, the meal was also larger than normal. He assumed the Saigos both knew about his upcoming liaison and therefore wanted to be sure he had the required stamina. This thought only served to heighten his excitement over what lay ahead for him.

Not long after Mrs. Saigo came to take away the dinner remains, Hamish saw a jinrikisha pull into the courtyard, from the guesthouse steps where he was waiting anxiously. As the runner pulled the vehicle up to the guesthouse, its yellow hanging lantern bobbed in the darkness.

The runner assisted a young woman as she stepped out of the jinrikisha and then quickly pulled the vehicle over to the carriage house – after which he squatted on the ground, apparently intending to wait until his passenger returned.

As she approached the guesthouse the young woman bowed deeply to Hamish and he bowed back. He then escorted her inside, after they had both removed their footwear. Once inside, in the light of the multiple candles he had lit in anticipation of her arrival, he examined her as discretely as he could. Her heavy white makeup caused her bright red lips and black hair to create a *jarring* visual effect, and made it impossible for him to determine if she were pretty or not. And a quick glance at her kimono, while it was superficially attractive, was obviously not of the high quality he had seen in the shop windows of the Ginza. In fact, it appeared to be of the same average quality as those back at the workshop Studio – used in photographs that attempted to illustrate Japanese daily life and customs.

After some additional deep bowing, the young woman danced around the small guesthouse for a time, slowly gliding her white stocking-covered feet over the tatami mats. Then she suddenly and sensuously pulled aside the folding screen which led to the sleeping area. She gracefully turned and, with a dainty hand, beckoned Hamish to join her there. He had been sitting cross-legged on the tatami while she danced.

With the greatest of expectations, he rose and followed her silent command. By the time he reached his sleeping pallet, she was already removing her kimono. Soon, she was completely naked. Then she lay down on the pallet, on her back, with legs spread apart.

At first, Hamish was dumb-founded, for while such brazen behavior was the rule of business at the Morton Street bordello, he had expected the geisha experience to reflect the reticence and subtlety he had experienced among the Japanese people since his arrival.

The young woman, with outstretched arms, beckoned him to join her. Instinctively, he undressed, mounted her, and within a very short time it was all over. She quickly left the pallet, dressed, bowed deeply one last time and rushed down the steps of the guesthouse after retrieving her wooden clogs on the porch. The jinrikisha runner came to her promptly, she entered his conveyance, and they disappeared through the courtyard gate – into the dark night.

Hamish returned to his pallet, after snuffing out all the candles he had previously lit. He found himself somewhat disoriented, and pondered what had just transpired. *Was this the awesome geisha experience men talked about? It's no different than a quick poke with Maisie back home!*

These frustrating thoughts were foremost in his mind as he fell asleep later – confused and unfulfilled.

TWELVE

Several days after Hamish received the gift of the geisha, he was still somewhat disturbed over the events of that evening. Rarely in his life had an occasion so anticipated been so disappointing.

On this particular morning, he was trying to drive that thought from his mind by assisting the *talkative* Card Shop clerk who had originally told him about the Belgian business partner of the Prince. He and the clerk had earlier finished re-arranging items in the display window – including the placement of new postcard products and recent portraits. Now they were stocking the shop's shelves and counters in a manner they hoped would make the merchandise more-easily visible and appealing to visitors.

At one point, Hamish happened to glance at the window and immediately stopped what he was doing, transfixed. Standing in the street, peering closely at the goods on display in the window, was the most beautiful creature he had ever seen. He quickly realized it was a young *man* – perhaps twenty-years of age, although he was aware that he had difficulty estimating the ages of Japanese individuals.

Although he could only view the young gentleman from the waist up, he realized he was not wearing Western-style clothing. Rather, he wore a dark blue, simple traditional kimono – covered with a white pattern resembling pairs of birds' wings. Also, his head was completely shaved, which further drew attention to his handsome – no, *beautiful* countenance.

A few minutes later, the young man opened the door to the Card Shop. He stood in the doorway momentarily – wooden clogs in hand, obviously looking for a place to leave them. When he noticed the floor was covered with stone rather than wood or tatami mats, he replaced the clogs on his white stocking-covered feet.

The visitor then entered, bowed to the clerk and Hamish, and began to speak in Japanese to the former individual. Hamish understood nothing that was being said, but after a brief conversation with the gentleman, the clerk knocked on the closed door of the Prince's office and then went inside.

During the brief time he was gone, Hamish stole glances at this incredible creature, until he felt the growing member inside his trousers and quickly turned away in embarrassment. He then proceeded to pretend he was re-arranging merchandise on the shelves.

Suddenly the office door burst open and the Prince came rushing out – more animated than Hamish had ever seen him. He bowed deeply to the visitor, who responded in kind, and then they both disappeared behind the closed door.

Hamish had never seen the Prince fawn over a visitor in this manner, and then he recalled that Kashiwara was eagerly awaiting a response from the Royal Palace – to his offer to provide complimentary portraits of the Emperor and the Royal Family. *Perhaps this gentleman has come with the Emperor's response?* He wondered.

Hamish also recalled the effort the Prince had put

• The Meiji Prince •

into that invitation. He hired a professional calligrapher to write it out in a most artistic manner – on a small parchment scroll. Then he took it to a professional gift-wrapper, who selected a narrow wooden box, and covered it with rich brocade. A thin gift card, also designed by the calligrapher, was placed on top of the brocaded box, and then pure silk ribbons were used to tie the card in place.

Before he could ask the talkative clerk who the visitor was, the young man anticipated his question, eager to show Hamish how knowledgeable he was on matters pertaining to Japanese society.

"That is Hiro, Page to the famous retired samurai, Toshiro – who is his *tatsujin*, his *Master*."

"Who?" Hamish asked.

"Hiro – the Page to samurai Toshiro. He desires to have his portrait taken, and as you know, Prince Kashiwara must interview all such clients to determine if they will be photographed here or at the villa. *You* will undoubtedly be given the assignment for this very important commission, at the villa."

Hamish was still confused. "Why is this young man so important?" He asked.

"*He* is not so important – his *Master* is – the famous samurai Toshiro."

"I reckon I'm not clear on the *samurai*. Can you tell me a mite bit about them?"

The clerk then proudly, but briefly, related some of Japan's glorious history to this *barbarian* – although he and his colleagues would never openly use such a term in Hamish's presence. At home, however, his elderly grandparents – who never reconciled themselves to the arrival of Commodore Perry and his *black ships*, used the insulting phrase frequently.

"The samurai were the elite, traditional warrior

class of Japan – especially powerful under the Tokugawa Shogunate. Master Toshiro's ancestors were hereditary samurai and accumulated a degree of wealth over many years – some of which has been passed down to him. This has allowed him to live in a beautiful small villa, in near seclusion with his Page, now that the Emperor has outlawed the samurai as a symbol of *old* Japan."

Hamish was surprisingly intrigued by the story the clerk was telling him. Somehow he had not heard this history earlier. Without prompting, the clerk continued his recitation.

"The Emperor forced them to surrender their swords – which they consider their *souls,* and to cut off the symbolic topknot on their shaved heads. They may also not wear their elaborate samurai warrior battle dress in public. There is currently much tension between them and the Meiji Government – which sees them as stubborn reactionaries who refuse to accept the movement toward modernization, through the adoption of Western ways."

"And what of Master Toshiro?" Hamish asked. "Why is *he* so important, if these warriors are out-of-favor at the Palace?"

"Ah," the clerk replied, "Toshiro's family was so powerful, for so long, that the Emperor accepted a daring compromise Toshiro put forth to him. The Court were stunned to learn that Toshiro was so bold as to send a missive to the Emperor in which he agreed to cut off his topknot and abandon his samurai dress – but pleaded he be allowed to retain his samurai swords, both the long one and the short one. He further offered never to take them beyond the walls of his villa. He argued that the swords were centuries-old family treasures – actually *spiritual* objects presented to him by his ancestors. After much reported debate over the matter at Court, the Emperor agreed – to the surprise of many. This was viewed as an indication of the power Master Toshiro still holds, even in the Meiji era."

"Did the Emperor offer a reason for granting this gent such a mighty honor?" Hamish asked.

"The Emperor does not have to *justify* his decisions – he is, after all, *God*. However, he is said to have viewed Toshiro's having taken English lessons, as soon as tutors arrived here, as a sign that he will eventually fall in line with the modernization program."

Just then, Kashiwara's door opened and he and the Page emerged. The Prince appeared to be beside himself, bowing repeatedly to his visitor. Then he turned to Hamish and introduced him to Hiro. He explained that the young man was interested in having a portrait made and they had just reviewed some of Hamish's best work. He further announced that an agreement had been reached that on the following afternoon, Hiro would arrive at the villa after lunch, to have his portrait taken by Hamish. And since he knew only a little English, and Hamish knew even less Japanese, Mr. Saigo would be present to translate when necessary. After more bowing, Hiro left and the Prince beckoned Hamish to come into his office.

Behind the closed door, Kashiwara gushed over this commission. "This is almost the next best thing to an Imperial portrait sitting," he exclaimed, "for Toshiro is so famous and respected throughout Tokyo, the mere fact that his Page will be photographed by you – obviously with his Master's permission, will likely bring more high-class clients to us. Word of such an event will travel quickly in the best of circles – I will see to that. You *must* do everything you can to make him feel comfortable tomorrow, and to produce a portrait of great beauty – although in *this* case, that should not be difficult. I'm sure you agree."

Hamish was uncomfortable with the latter remark and quickly turned away from it.

"You say he speaks little English, Purinsu?"

"Yes, but as I said earlier, Mr. Saigo will assist in the translation. However, I believe it will be most politic and polite if you learn and use a few basic Japanese words tomorrow – words you surely have heard in your weeks of residence here. I can think of at least three simple phrases which will likely assist you through the encounter, while Mr. Saigo relays posing instructions to Hiro: *konnichiwa* – good afternoon, when he arrives; *domo arigato* – thank you, when the portrait sitting is over; and *sayonara* – goodbye, upon his departure. Are you comfortable with those, Mr. Boyd?"

Hamish nodded, having heard those phrases repeatedly in recent weeks, and even having used them occasionally.

The next morning, Hamish was filled with anticipation of Hiro's pending arrival after lunch. He kept changing the background scenery for the portrait – adding and then taking away items – chairs, plinths, painted folding screens, vases of silk flowers. Finally he decided that the sitter's beauty, in and of itself, should be the focus. He then decided that the portrait would be taken in front of a plain shoji sliding wall, with Hiro resting his elbow on the simplest plinth he had at the villa studio. And to be certain he would end up with a satisfactory result, two exposures would be taken, one with Hiro resting his right elbow on the plinth, the other while resting his left there. In both instances, his extraordinary countenance would be the focus for viewers fortunate to gaze upon the final result.

When the jinrikisha later entered the courtyard, Hiro emerged wearing a simple, but beautiful, white kimono covered with a small red design which Hamish did not recognize. Later, Mr. Saigo told him it was symbolic of the *loyalty* due to a master, by his servant.

The prerequisite bows and verbal greetings were made, and then Hamish positioned Hiro at the plinth. Mr. Saigo explained the process, and stressed that he *must* remain perfectly still during the plate's exposure, until Hamish told him he could relax.

During the first exposure, Hamish was so taken by his subject's beauty, once again his member started to swell in his trousers. He tried to hide the protuberance, as best he could, behind the tripod. He feared it was still visible when he later came forward to reposition Hiro so that his other elbow rested on the plinth.

After two exposures had been made, he felt secure that at least one of them would yield acceptable results, although he could not imagine such a flawless creature not photographing well under any conditions.

Upon completion of the portrait-taking, Hiro was instructed regarding when the finished photographs could be retrieved at the workshop. And then, with *domo arigatos* and *sayonaras* all around, Hiro left in the waiting jinrikisha.

After Hamish thanked Mr. Saigo for his assistance, he rushed to his darkroom. Rarely had he ever been so anxious to see the results of his work, having already decided to print an extra copy of each pose – for his personal *pleasure*.

THIRTEEN

On the appointed day, an elderly, bent-over gentleman arrived at the workshop with a note from Hiro. It identified the bearer as *Mr. Ohsugi*, Master Toshiro's household servant, sent to retrieve Hiro's portraits.

Upon being shown the note, written in Japanese characters, the Prince treated the old man with great courtesy, and after mutual bowing and verbal greetings, handed him the photographs – elaborately wrapped.

After he left, the Prince explained to Hamish that Mr. Ohsugi had been a fierce samurai warrior in his day, but like so many others who had little in the way of personal fortune, he was left destitute after the Meiji Government outlawed the open practice of his profession. Many such as he were reduced to the status of beggars – but Master Toshiro hired Ohsugi to be his household servant, out of respect and recognition for his heroic past.

As Hamish listened to Ohsugi's story, he found himself intrigued – and somewhat overwhelmed, by the complex society in which he now found himself. Therefore, he was filled with surprise and anticipation when, several days later, Mr. Ohsugi returned with an invitation – written in *English*, requesting his presence at Master Toshiro's villa for tea, two afternoons later. When he showed it to the Prince, the latter was overcome with delight.

"Rarely is anyone allowed inside Toshiro's villa! You must observe carefully and report every detail back to me. And apply all the courtesy and respect you can summon up for the occasion – for it may lead to the great honor of being asked to photograph *him*."

Thus it was with considerable excitement that Hamish entered the jinrikisha sent by Master Toshiro to the Prince's villa at the appointed time, two days later. And when he quickly reached his host's villa, he realized it was in the same district of Tokyo as that of the Prince – less than fifteen minutes away, according to his pocket watch.

The runner waited while Hamish walked up to the large wooden door set into the villa's high walls. A bronze chain hung beside the door, and when Hamish pulled on it, he realized it was connected to a bell on the other side of the wall. Soon, a small wooden door panel slid open, revealing Hiro's face peering out, and reminding Hamish of a beautiful *framed* portrait. Upon seeing him, Hiro nodded, closed the panel, and unlocked the large door.

As Hamish stood in the doorway, Hiro bowed to him, and then went over to the runner. He handed him some money, and spoke briefly with him in Japanese. It occurred to Hamish that he was arranging for his return trip to the Prince's villa, later.

Hiro then led Hamish into the courtyard, after which he turned and bolted the door. Unlike the courtyard at the Prince's villa, Hamish noted that they were in a beautiful garden of modest size, where carriages and other conveyances could not be accommodated. It would be some days later before Hamish learned there was an alley behind the villa where

Toshiro's small carriage and his old warhorse were stabled.

His eyes were immediately drawn to his left, where a beautiful tree in full bloom stood proudly – surrounded by short shrubs of various kinds. In the midst of this tranquil setting was a small pond, with several large *koi* languidly swimming in circles – their orange-gold bodies glistening in the mid-afternoon sunlight.

Hamish then turned to his right. In the corner where the front and side walls obscuring the villa met, was a large stone lantern, placed in front of some tall bamboo. In front of the lantern were several varieties of stones – differing in size, shape and color, which had been raked into wavy patterns. The whole sensual and aesthetic experience of the garden almost lulled him into a dream-like state. But then he heard low grunting from the area where the villa itself was situated. When he looked in that direction, the contrast with what he saw and felt in the garden was dramatic.

Standing at the bottom of the villa's porch steps was a sturdy gentleman, on the short size – as most Japanese appeared to Hamish, wearing a black kimono covered with a silver-gray circular pattern. At that moment, Hamish realized that Hiro's garment was of the same color and design, however the circles on his kimono were smaller.

The other gentleman, who Hamish assumed to be the samurai, Toshiro, was deep in concentration as he struck various fierce poses while waving a *short* sword about. Hamish had no idea how long he had been at this exercise, but soon the samurai pointed his sword downward – toward the earth. Hiro then rushed over to him, bowed, and took the sword from him. After bowing again, he placed it in a box which was lying on the villa's narrow porch. He then approached Toshiro again, bowed, and used a small towel to gently wipe the perspiration from his face. After bowing once more, he returned the towel to a wooden tray on the porch, and retrieved a *long* sword. A final bow was made and then Hiro joined Hamish, who stood nearby watching Toshiro perform a series of stylized thrusts and parries with the new weapon.

After a time, Toshiro pointed the sword toward the earth, Hiro rushed over to take it, and the previous formal sequence was repeated. After the long sword had been returned to the box, and Toshiro's face was once again towel-dried by his Page, he looked in Hamish's direction. To Hamish, Toshiro appeared to be coming out of a trance, staring at his visitor for a time before walking over and stopping about six feet away.

The samurai stiffly bowed to Hamish, who returned the gesture. And then, just as Hamish was about to say *Konnichiwa*, Toshiro greeted him with the words, "Good afternoon, Mr. Hamish Boyd."

Caught off guard, and a bit flustered, Hamish managed to respond, "Good afternoon, Master Toshiro."

"We may speak English while you are here – I learned it as soon as tutors were available. It is a samurai principle to learn as much as one can of the enemy – and the intrusive American *black ships* in our harbor were certainly viewed by those in my profession as alien and dangerous upon their appearance in our reclusive world."

Hamish was confused, not knowing how to respond – *the enemy?*

"I never reckoned we were enemies, Master."

"Ah, Mr. Hamish Boyd – sadly I believe that one

day our two great nations will be at war with each other."

Hamish thought for a moment, and then recalling his previous encounters with exotic, mysterious aspects of Japanese life, responded, "Is it because our nations are so *different*, Master?"

Toshiro stared directly into his eyes for what appeared to be a long time, making Hamish self-conscious and uncomfortable. Finally, he spoke.

"No, Mr. Hamish Boyd. When that sad day arrives, it will be because our nations are so *similar* – so much alike."

Toshiro, who was well-trained in the art of reading that which is in the hearts and minds of men, realized his guest was confused and uncomfortable with this subject, and quickly turned the conversation elsewhere.

"But I have invited you for tea – please come into my humble home while I prepare it. I do not have a separate teahouse, as does Kashiwara – is that not so?"

Hamish quickly responded, "The Purinsu has a mighty fine teahouse *and* guesthouse."

"Is that what he tells you to call him – *Purinsu*?"

"Yes, Master Toshiro, or *Prince Kashiwara*, if I prefer."

The samurai thought for a moment and then appeared to speak with deliberation.

"I beg your pardon, Mr. Hamish Boyd, but I shall call your employer simply, *Kashiwara*. In truth, he is no more a *Prince* than I."

"He isn't?" Hamish asked, perplexed. "Even the Japanese Consulate official in San Francisco called him *that* when he hired me in his stead."

Master Toshiro appeared to ponder this news for

a moment, and then he asked, "Do you recall the name of the Consulate staff member who represented Kashiwara on his quest for your services?"

Hamish slowly responded, "His name was.....oh yes, Mr. Hasegawa, I believe."

"Ah," the samurai replied, "the Kashiwara and the Hasegawa clans are distantly related. Clan loyalty would likely have been behind Mr. Hasegawa's actions. If the Emperor knew, he would likely have been displeased, in view of his repugnance toward Kashiwara in the past."

"The Emperor is unhappy with my employer?" Hamish asked, now sounding more fearful than inquisitive.

"If I may be candid, Mr. Hamish Boyd – your employer is not a Prince of the Royal Family. He is a distant – very distant, *Cousin* to the Emperor. He offended His Majesty by once requesting a stipend paid only to closely-related members of the Royal Family. But worse was yet to come. Still believing himself of Royal birth, he dared send a proposal of marriage to the Imperial Palace, requesting the hand of one of the Royal Princesses when she became of age. This was a great breach of protocol, in view of the strict lineage of Royal marriages."

After a time, Hamish asked, "But how can he call himself a *Prince*, then?"

"He was sent a message to cease doing so, but he continued – in his business dealings with foreigners, most likely to impress them. Word of this reached the Court of course, and rumor has it that the Emperor has come to tolerate this questionable behavior in the hope that if Kashiwara becomes wealthy as a result, there will be less chance he will ever approach the Court again for a Royal stipend."

"I'm *graveled* by this. I guess I was *gulled* into believing he was a genuine Prince – the first I ever was to meet in all my born days," Hamish muttered, forlornly.

Master Toshiro was unfamiliar with San Francisco slang, but recognizing Hamish's disappointment in what had just been revealed, quickly responded.

"Regardless of his immodesty, since he is your employer – your *Master*, you must address him as he pleases. If he desires to be called *Purinsu*, then you *must* do so. For my part, he is simply *Kashiwara*. By the way, you may call me simply *Toshiro* if you like, as I am not your Master. And I shall call you *Mr. Hamish Boyd*. If we should later come to know each other better, there are Japanese expressions which are less formal and which I may employ in addressing you. But now, let me invite you into my humble home for tea."

After Hamish removed his shoes on the porch, and the others removed their wooden clogs, all three entered into a modest room, furnished in traditional Japanese style. Then, as Master Toshiro began to kneel on the tatami, he spoke to Hamish.

"You may sit cross-legged if you like, Mr. Hamish Boyd. I am aware that Westerners are uncomfortable kneeling – not being used to the position from early childhood, as are we."

"That's mighty kind of you, Toshiro. My legs do cramp if I kneel too long. Sitting wild-Injun style suits me just fine."

Toshiro was about to let that statement pass, but his curiosity got the better of him. "What is *wild-Injun*, please?"

Hamish blushed a bit before replying – which happened frequently in view of his pale skin and blond features. "They're the Indians out our way. They can get a bit ferocious at times, so we call them *wild*."

Toshiro reflected on this and then he asked, "Are they not the original inhabitants of the land Americans now occupy? Some even believe they originated in Asia."

"Well, yes – but they needed taming by the white man. They are…..were…..*savages*."

Restraining himself, Toshiro responded, "I see." Then he continued, hoping he wasn't being rude to his first-time foreign guest.

"*The Frenchman* had much to say on this matter."

"Who?" Hamish asked.

"The Frenchman."

"Oh, you mean *The Belgian* who is Prince Kashiwara's business partner in Europe?"

Toshiro smiled. "No, I speak of the inquisitive and perceptive gentleman from France who several decades ago traveled to your country and wrote insightfully about what he saw and heard – Alexis de Tocqueville. Have you not heard of him? I assumed all obviously-educated Americans such as yourself, had."

Hamish's face turned a deeper red this time. "No, Sir. I only studied the *3-Rs* and photography – just what I needed to make a living."

"The *3-Rs*?"

"Pardon – *reading, 'riting and 'rithmetic*. Along with photography, they were all I needed to know to make a living."

"I see. So the history of your nation is not of relevance?"

"Not in making a living, I reckon."

"When I studied English, the tutors were asked

by we Japanese students to employ reading material which would acquaint us with the *history* of America and Europe. That is how I came to read some of de Tocqueville's work on your country. He was especially concerned with the treatment, by the white settlers, of the native inhabitants they found on the land they confiscated."

"Begging your pardon, Sir, but I believe there were fair treaties drawn up for land purchases."

"Were there? Are you sure, Mr. Hamish Boyd?"

"Well, so's I've been told."

"But you have not *studied* the history of the matter, I take it?"

"No – as I said, I only know what it takes to make a living – and history isn't necessary for *that*."

"Then allow me to leave you with a thought to ponder at your leisure: many ancient scholars believed that while history may not prepare one to *make a living*, it does prepare one for *how to live*. And now, let us have our tea."

Toshiro then nodded at Hiro, who brought forth a small low table, upon which he placed a plain glass vase. He then returned with a reed basket containing greenery and blossoms. After examining the vase from all sides, and the way the light coming through the open shoji was reflected by it, Toshiro selected several pieces of greenery. He held them at various angles and scrutinized them closely. Then he put a single piece in the vase – shifting it several times before he apparently was satisfied. He did the same thing with a single long-stemmed yellow flower he selected from the basket. After what appeared to Hamish to be an inordinate amount of time, Toshiro was satisfied with the result and signaled to Hiro to remove the debris. Afterward, Hiro brought forth the items for preparing tea.

Hamish watched, transfixed, as this alleged former fierce warrior – still obviously skilled in swordsmanship, now gingerly went through the ancient tea-preparation ritual, which had its roots in Zen Buddhism. Each item – tea bowls, bamboo tea whisk, tea scoop, hot pads, and the tea caddy – was wiped with a small silk cloth. Hot water and tea powder were mixed together with the whisk, after which a cup of the brew was passed among the three of them. A small cloth accompanied the cup, with which to wipe it before being passed on.

The contrast for Hamish, with tea preparation and consumption back home in San Francisco, could not have been greater. When all the tea was consumed in this manner, every utensil was carefully washed by Toshiro and then stored by Hiro in a nearby low cabinet. Then Toshiro turned to Hamish.

"And what do you think of our custom, Mr. Hamish Boyd?"

"Honestly, I'm quite *graveled*. I never thought a warrior would be making tea and arranging flowers, Toshiro."

"I see. But the *order* I brought to these domestic tasks is in keeping with the *spiritual discipline* central to the warrior class. It is not unrelated to the concentration I apply when engaged in swordplay. Do you know the definition of *samurai*, Mr. Hamish Boyd?"

With increasing discomfort, and with regret that he ever raised the issue of his perceived discrepancies between Toshiro's behavior and his reputation, Hamish sheepishly replied, "No, Sir."

Slowly, deliberately, Toshiro concisely answered, "*samurai is the way of the pen and the sword.*"

Hamish's confusion and embarrassment at this moment were once again evident on his flushed face. And so, Toshiro continued, in a patient, didactic manner.

"Everything we do *here and now* is rooted in our historical past and tradition – that which tells us *how to live*. Much comes from Buddhism – particularly the *Zen* sect, but there is something we owe to *Taoism*, which may also be relevant to this conversation. I refer to the *yin* and the *yang*. Taoism views the universe as made up of these two complimentary principles. The former is the *female principle*, the latter the *male*. They are combined in *all* things – even in the actions of samurai warriors!"

With that, Toshiro flashed a broad smile and made a small chuckle. Any tension that had been palpable in the atmosphere now seemed to vanish. And so, Hamish smiled broadly in return – although he still did not fully understand his conversation with Toshiro on this visit. And then, Toshiro spoke once more.

"Hiro has signaled that it is nearly time for the jinrikisha runner to collect you. Before you go, I must tell you I have found our conversation today very interesting. I would therefore like you to return soon – in particular to discuss the portraits you created of my Page. Can you come again in two days?"

"That will be *Monday*. Yes – I can come on Monday. I only go to the Purinsu's workshop on Wednesdays, Thursdays and Fridays."

"Very well. I shall see you at the same time. A jinrikisha will be sent to collect you, as was done today."

By the time he returned to the Kashiwara villa, Hamish was certain of two things: he would never let the Prince know what he learned on this day of his personal history in relation to the Imperial Family, *and* he had likely met the most fascinating person he ever would – in his entire lifetime.

FOURTEEN

As the jinrikisha runner took Hamish back to Toshiro's villa the following Monday, he recalled how eager the Prince had been – on Saturday evening, to learn everything he could of his initial visit to the reclusive, retired samurai.

"Did he request his portrait be taken?" was Kashiwara's first anxious query.

When Hamish responded that Toshiro had not, the Prince frowned. However, when told that Toshiro had invited him back to discuss Hiro's portraits, Kashiwara's hopes again rose. He was convinced that such a commission would represent a great coup – to be exploited when word of it spread throughout the upper societal levels of Tokyo. But when he repeated this refrain to Hamish several times, his employee indicated some doubt.

"How can our dealings with Toshiro become known far and wide, right-quick, Purinsu?"

Kashiwara smiled indulgently. "Ah, Mr. Boyd, you have apparently failed to notice that every jinrikisha runner has two eyes with which to see, two ears with which to hear – and two *hands* with which to accept a few yen now and then for information concerning the comings and goings of parties of interest. *That* is how one knows each time Toshiro decides to make one of his rare visits to his wife and children in Kyoto."

• The Meiji Prince •

Hamish visibly appeared surprised, and Kashiwara continued.

"You did not know he has a wife and children – two to be precise, a son and a daughter?"

"No, Sir. I reckoned he lived alone with his Page and his servant."

Kashiwara grinned, and replied with a hint of the sardonic in his voice.

"It is precisely because of the profound intimacy Toshiro shares with his Page that his wife retreated to her mother's home in Kyoto, several years ago. To his credit, he is rumored to send her funds on a regular basis, for his family's support."

While Hamish pondered this unexpected information, Kashiwara changed the subject to that of the samurai's *home*. Hamish reluctantly provided a rather vague description of the premises, emphasizing the traditional, spare Japanese décor maintained by Toshiro. Appearing satisfied for the time being, Kashiwara raised another issue.

"And what did you talk about during your visit, if not photography?"

"He wanted to talk about *America* – asked me questions about my country's history. It was mighty embarrassing, because he's read more history about the United States than I have!"

Kashiwara appeared to be amused by this latter remark, and then ended the conversation by again urging Hamish to steer Monday's forthcoming meeting toward the subject of a portrait commission.

For Hamish, this conversation with Kashiwara was awkward. He did not want to betray Toshiro's privacy to this *bogus* Prince, to whom he must continue to appear gulled into believing his Royal *conceit* – but he also realized an employee owes a degree of loyalty to his employer. The extent to which he would allow himself to prove that loyalty by detailing what occurred during his visits to Toshiro's villa, was at the heart of his dilemma.

But these thoughts were put aside when Hamish arrived at the samurai's villa, and was soon sitting cross-legged once again in the room where tea had been served two days earlier.

"I thought that today I would serve *sake* – our native rice wine. Would that be acceptable to you, Mr. Hamish Boyd?" Toshiro asked.

"Oh yes, Toshiro. Sake is mighty fine."

Hiro brought forth a porcelain flask, filled with sake, and three small cups. All four pieces were bright red in color, and helped create a somewhat festive ambiance on this occasion.

After several cups of sake were consumed in near-silence, Toshiro spoke.

"And now let us examine the portraits you produced of my Page."

Hiro rose and retrieved a small bamboo easel from behind a folding screen, upon which the portraits were displayed side-by-side. All three stared at the portraits for a time, and then Toshiro spoke.

"Since the 8th century, artists in Japan have focused on *beauty*, and the desire to discover the *beautiful essence* in objects. Do you believe you have accomplished that with these photographic portraits, Mr. Hamish Boyd?"

Once again, Hamish's face was momentarily flushed with scarlet, as he struggled to compose an intelligent response to his obviously-learnéd host. When he eventually answered, it was awkwardly, and with some hesitation.

"Well….I…..er, I reckon the portraits *are* beautiful."

"Of course, Mr. Hamish Boyd – but is that not

solely because the *subject* is beautiful? But as *works of art*, are they beautiful?"

"I reckon so, Toshiro," Hamish replied – with less conviction than he had hoped to project.

"Hiro tells me you look into a hole in a box, squeeze a bulb and order the subject to remain still while you capture the image on a glass plate. Does *that* process make your photographs true works of art?"

Trying to sound positive, Hamish responded, "Well, Sir, I believe so – I had to devise the poses for the subject, arrange the background scene – all for the final composition."

"When *I* look at these portraits, I see a simple shoji screen in the background, and in one instance Hiro looks to his left, in the other to his right. Is this the artistic component of which you speak?"

Quietly, Hamish muttered, "I reckon so."

"The problem I have with this new *photography*, Mr. Hamish Boyd, is that art – like life, should be a *journey*, but I see *no* journey here. Suddenly one is *there*, but one does not know how the artist reached his destination."

Hamish was now visibly uncomfortable. "I'm a mite vexed, Toshiro – graveled. I never did think of photographs as anything but *art*."

Toshiro paused for a moment and then said something to Hiro in Japanese. Hiro left the room and quickly returned with a scroll. Toshiro unrolled it and set it on the tatami mat, beside Hamish.

"What do you see, Mr. Hamish Boyd?" He asked.

"I see a painting – delicate, of a garden, with a figure standing in it."

"Do you see anything else?"

"Well, I reckon the colors are soothing, mighty soft – almost *pretty*."

Toshiro let out a soft sigh.

"Do you not see the artist's *journey* here? It is present in every visible brushstroke, added over the course of time – days, weeks, perhaps even months. That *journey* is what I do not see in your photographs."

Hamish didn't know how to respond. Toshiro continued.

"What do you understand of the human figure in this painting?"

Hamish peered closely, and then responded. "I believe it is a *man* – no, a *woman* – no!"

"So you are uncertain of the figure's gender?"

"Uh....it looks like a strong man because it is standing so mighty erect. And yet, there is something in the way the body is a mite turned that almost looks delicate – *feminine*."

Toshiro grinned. "Do you recall our discussion during your previous visit regarding the *yin and the yang*? Is it possible the artist has captured that here? After all, the figure's facial features have been deliberately undefined – adding to the air of mystery inherent in the work."

"I reckon so," Hamish responded, sheepishly.

"So, I believe you can now see why I consider this painting a work of art, and photography merely a *technique*. Your photographs are *literal* – they only reveal Hiro's superficial features, but not his *soul*. But in this painting, we are invited to speculate on his soul, rather than focus upon the essence of a fixed photographic moment in time."

"The figure in the painting is of Hiro, your Page?"

"Precisely – and *I* am the artist who has tried to capture his soul, and not only his admittedly-superficial physical beauty."

Hamish reached for his sake cup and drained its

contents, after which Hiro quickly refilled it. His flushed face revealed his lack of a clever rebuttal, and frustrated him – but he could think of nothing further to say at the time. However, Toshiro appeared to be compelled to ensure he had the *last* word on the matter.

"I do not believe the Japanese people will ever widely accept your Western photography, in place of the wonder of watercolors and other traditional forms of painting."

Emboldened by the sake, Hamish responded, more firmly than he had in the past.

"I reckon the spread of photography is inevitable, Toshiro. Already the *dry plate process* is on the horizon and photographs will become faster and cheaper to produce. And the images created will be those folks desire to have in their houses, in right-handy albums on the parlor table."

"Perhaps time will prove you right, Mr. Hamish Boyd. In the meantime, let me emphasize that I have truly enjoyed our little talks and wish to make them a twice-weekly event – on Saturdays and Mondays. Will that suit you?"

Relieved that their obvious disagreement over the merits of photography was not going to be divisive, Hamish responded with alacrity.

"I would be most honored, Toshiro – as long as my employer does not require my service at those times."

"Of course, *Hamish-san*."

Upon hearing this new form of address, Hamish stared at Toshiro momentarily – and the latter anticipated his thoughts.

"I need no longer address you in such a formal manner, as *Mr. Hamish Boyd*. I now believe we have rather quickly reached such a level of comradeship that we may follow the Japanese custom for indicating such – by the addition of *san* after one's name. Thus, you will be *Hamish-san*, and I shall be *Toshiro-san*. Are you comfortable with this?"

"Yes.....Toshiro-san," Hamish replied, with a grin and a sense of relief, after what he viewed as a tense discussion of the merits of photography versus painting.

"Good! But before you leave, Hiro will prepare a note, written in Japanese characters. On one side it will direct jinrikisha runners you encounter in the street near your employer's villa, to bring you here. And on the other side, it will direct them to return you there from my villa. I assume you will agree this will be a very efficient way to arrange your transportation back-and-forth."

"That's mighty thoughtful, Toshiro-san."

"Also, when you come next time, please bring several of the woodcut print postcards Kashiwara sells. They will provide for *more* interesting conversation."

More sake was consumed in silence while Hiro carefully and artistically prepared the note for the jinrikisha runners, using black ink and a brush. While he did so, Hamish stared at Toshiro's painting of Hiro in the garden. Try as he might, he failed to see its superiority to his own stunning photographs of the Page. *Do they really only capture his surface beauty, as Toshiro claims?*

FIFTEEN

As expected, Kashiwara was most anxious to learn if Toshiro now desired to have his portrait taken. And as also expected he was disappointed when Hamish told him Toshiro not only did *not* request a portrait sitting, but had spent their visit extolling the superiority of painting over photography. However, when Hamish revealed that Toshiro desired twice-weekly visits from the Prince's American employee – to discuss heaven knows what, Kashiwara brightened.

"Even if he takes awhile to request a portrait, the mere fact that you will be seen frequently going to and coming from his villa will arouse curiosity among those who have never entered that walled sanctuary. And that information alone will be good for my business," Kashiwara concluded.

And so, with his employer's blessing, Hamish relaxed and looked forward to seeing Toshiro frequently during his remaining time in Japan. As a result, he was quite enthusiastic as he arrived for his next visit, bringing several of the Prince's woodblock print postcards, as requested.

"Will sake do, today?" Toshiro asked, after he, Hamish and Hiro were seated on the tatami.

"Yes, thank you, Toshiro-san."

After Hiro served the wine from the same bright-red sake set as previously, Toshiro began the day's discussion.

"May I see the woodblock print postcards you brought from Kashiwara's Card Shop?"

After Hamish passed them to him, Toshiro examined the postcards carefully for some time, and then spoke.

"Since the 18th century, polychrome woodblock prints have been very popular in Japan. There have been several artists of the medium who are now highly esteemed among those of us who appreciate the long, complex process required to produce such works of art. They include *Ando Hiroshige*, who is my personal favorite. Allow me to show you some of his work." Toshiro then nodded at Hiro, who retrieved several prints from a nearby cabinet.

Toshiro continued, "Hiroshige's most renowned work, completed approximately twenty years ago, was *One Hundred Views of Edo*. Now, of course, one speaks of *Tokyo*, as you know. Here are some examples of his work. What do you think of them?"

Hamish took the prints in hand and attempted to study them as diligently as had Toshiro when he examined Kashiwara's products. One of the prints was a waterway scene, the other a snow scene. Finally, Hamish said, "They are restful – and very detailed."

"Yes," Toshiro responded, "one may say *that*. Perhaps if we place them side-by-side with the ones you brought today from Kashiwara's inventory, you will have *more* to offer."

Hamish stared at the prints and then felt confident in sounding authoritative. "Hiroshige's are more delicate – the colors are more subtle, and the composition more balanced."

"Exactly, Hamish-san! I agree with you completely. But unfortunately, those features of traditional Japanese art are rapidly disappearing in this era of *Westernization*. Now the colors are too bold everywhere, like this sake set which Hiro purchased in the Ginza, when I sent him there to buy it last year. I was curious to see if changes were occurring in the area of ceramic art as well. In earlier times, a sake set would have been decorated with the palest of background color, and perhaps minimal over-painted decorative design."

"I see," Hamish replied, nodding – happy to have said something with which Toshiro agreed. The latter continued.

"And of course the *subject* of the prints has changed. Hiroshige depicted the old, peaceful Edo. Now *modern Tokyo* is the preferred subject – Western-style hotels instead of inns, steamships in the harbor, Victorian commercial buildings. Would you believe the current Government actually *censors* these prints? Pre-approval from the censors is required before public sales may occur. This is because art is now to be in the service of the State – *not* the artist's vision."

Hamish looked appropriately dismayed, uncertain as to how openly-critical he should appear, as a foreign visitor in this land.

"And of course," Toshiro continued, "the drawings by Hiroshige and his fellow artists are much more refined than Kashiwara's crude, awkward and hastily-rendered compositions."

Hamish nodded in agreement, embarrassed somewhat at having once been impressed by his employer's merchandise.

Toshiro took back his prints, Hiro stored them and refilled the sake cups. Now visibly beaming over Hamish's absorption of the day's discussion, he decided to go further.

"Hamish-san, there is another category of woodblock prints – one created and sold outside the Government's purview. Are you familiar with our *floating world*?"

Hamish slowly shook his head from side-to-side.

"Then if I may, let me explain. The floating world is the world of entertainment, pleasure. And depicting it often features the activities of the *pleasure quarters* of our large cities. It is there that courtesans and prostitutes reign. Art works depicting that world are called *shunga* and are explicit, shall we say. As you might expect, there are many such prints whose subject is the floating world, often gathered into *pillowbooks*."

"Pillowbooks?"

"Yes – pillowbooks. These erotic books are usually kept in the sleeping quarters, as an instructive aid and stimulant for lovers. Or, for those times when one's lover is away and self-pleasure is the only recourse open to one. Do you understand?"

The scarlet color creeping across Hamish's face answered Toshiro's question, to his satisfaction. And so, he continued.

"Hiro will fetch one for you to examine," – and the Page quickly did so.

As Hamish turned the pages of the pillowbook, trying not to appear *too* interested, he was fascinated by the explicit nature of the various sex acts depicted. After a time, Toshiro spoke again.

"Do you not see that the same care – in terms of color, composition, detailed drawing has gone into these prints as those completed by estimable artists such as Hiroshige?"

Hamish had to nod in agreement, although the subject matter had now so stimulated him that once again, his erection was visibly pressing against his trousers and he could only hope that his host and Hiro had not noticed.

"And now," Toshiro continued, "allow me to show you some recent examples of shunga."

Hiro handed Hamish several woodblock print postcards, depicting sexually-explicit activities. Toshiro then asked, "Do you see a difference when these are compared with the others, Hamish-san?"

Hamish stammered a bit and then replied slowly, "The scenes on these postcards are more-crudely drawn. And the composition is not as artistic. And once again, the colors are garish."

"Precisely! These are but cheap imitations, aimed at the *foreign* market which views Japan as an exotic, colorful, garish nation. And so our exported woodblock prints – whether censored by the Government before shipment or sold clandestinely as these are, must be presented in this fashion to satisfy that fantasy about our nation and our lives. This is also the case with the ceramics prepared for export, as I mentioned earlier. Neither do they represent the authentic tradition of this nation as it was – and as it will one day be again!"

Hamish was somewhat frightened by the intensity with which the retired samurai delivered these pronouncements, and returned to drinking his sake in silence. Feeling pressed to say something on the subject, he muttered, "I have not seen such items for sale in the market."

"Of course not – they are sold *under the counter*, as we say. However, these garish postcard examples have been produced under your very nose."

Hamish's lower jaw dropped and his mouth opened. The frown on his face magnified his confusion. Toshiro was now ready to continue, with barely-concealed enthusiasm.

"These are products of Kashiwara's workshop – to be distributed and sold in Europe by his business associate who is known as The Belgian."

"What?" Hamish exclaimed.

"Yes, Hamish-san. In the evenings and on days when you are *not* about, they are printed at the workshop."

"But how does the Belgian gentleman pass them through *Customs* – both here and when he arrives in Europe?"

"They are very carefully packed – hidden among the conventional postcards Kashiwara produces. And also, *yen* are generously distributed to under-paid Customs officials here, and one assumes The Belgian uses local currency to pass his cargo through the inspection after landing in Europe. At any rate, the business arrangement between him and Kashiwara has been very satisfying for several years now and rumor has it such items attract high prices among European collectors of erotica."

Hamish listened quietly to this unsettling news, saying nothing as he continued to drain the sake cup which Hiro kept refilling. After a time, he spoke.

"Toshiro-san, how is it *you* know that which has been unknown to me since my arrival at the workshop?"

"Ah, Hamish-san – even though the world of the samurai is being forcibly pushed into the shadows by this Government, it continues to enjoy a network of familial relationships and comradeship, built up over the centuries. Thus – and I ask you *never* to reveal this to your employer, one of his employees in the Print Shop is none other than the grandson of Mr. Ohsugi, who you only know as my servant. What you do not know is that he was once a proud samurai warrior!"

"I see," Hamish replied with a nod – remembering what Kashiwara had previously told him in confidence about Ohsugi's samurai past.

"When you come next time," Toshiro then stated, while clearly indicating this visit was at an end, "please bring several of the photographic postcards you have helped Kashiwara produce. I am anxious to examine *your* views of Tokyo."

SIXTEEN

Hamish quickly summarized his most recent visit to Toshiro's villa, when questioned by Kashiwara upon his return.

"He was mighty anxious to talk about the fine old Japanese tradition of woodblock prints," Hamish offered Kashiwara. And then, in an attempt to raise his employer's spirits despite his continued failure to secure a portrait commission, he added a bit more.

"He was most praiseful of your efforts to keep the tradition alive by selling woodblock print postcards, here and abroad."

Evidently appeased, Kashiwara smiled and encouraged Hamish to continue the visits, and when Hamish arrived for the next one, he brought some of his photographic postcards – as Toshiro had requested.

After they were settled on the tatami and the sake had been poured, Hamish offered the postcards to his host. As before, Toshiro studied them closely, prior to responding.

"They depict a *very* different Tokyo from the *Edo* I once knew."

"It is the wish of my employer that I show *Westernized* Japan – as well as traditional views. He even told me recently that after I return home he is going to compile a beautiful album of my best pictures and send it to the Emperor. He expects His Majesty will be mighty pleased and even invite him to Court, for helping promote modern Meiji ideals."

Toshiro stared at Hamish as he said these words – and for so long thereafter that Hamish began to nervously shift his body while sitting in his customary cross-legged position. Finally, Toshiro spoke.

"Much Japanese thought is based upon the revelations of the Enlightened Buddha. I believe the time has now come, Hamish-san, for me to enlighten *you* as to why you have *really* been brought here by the opportunist, Kashiwara."

Hamish's body tensed upon hearing these words and his senses became heightened.

"Begging your pardon, Toshiro-san, but Kashiwara hired me to teach photography to his staff, in order to expand his postcard business beyond woodcut prints. I reckon it fits in with his interest in modern inventions."

Toshiro handed back Hamish's photographs and signaled to Hiro, who retrieved a small, plainly-wrapped brown paper packet from a nearby cabinet.

"Yes, Hamish-san, but not primarily for photographs such as those you have brought here today. Just as Kashiwara's most-profitable merchandise has been the shunga images he produces largely for the European market, so too *these* images will have already likely left with The Belgian as he sailed away recently."

Toshiro then handed the packet to Hamish and continued. "It is *these* photographs, not those which you brought here today, which are the *true* reason you were sent for by Kashiwara."

When Hamish opened the packet, he found a dozen or so photographic postcards – all depicting the most-explicit of sexual activities – performed by naked men and women. He threw a sharp glance in Toshiro's direction and then Hiro's, while the former urged him, "Study them closely before you speak, Hamish-san."

As Hamish stared at the images, with sufficient embarrassment for his pale face to redden, he concluded they depicted the variety of sexual acts also on display in the shunga pillowbooks to which Toshiro had introduced him. And then he noticed something which was particularly disquieting.

"Lord Almighty! The men in these pictures are the three assistants I taught my trade to!"

"Yes, Hamish-san," Toshiro offered, gently. "In the evenings and on days when you were not at the workshop, these three young men were instructed to photograph each other with common street prostitutes."

Hamish continued to stare at the images of the naked bodies of his young comrades, aware of the sprouting erection which was likely noticed by Toshiro and Hiro. But he made no attempt to conceal it, being preoccupied and confused over the actions of these polite, quiet young men – once assumed *innocent* – a view now obviously misguided and naïve. When he was able to collect his thoughts, he asked Toshiro a question.

"How did you come by these, Toshiro-san?"

"As with Kashiwara's shunga images, I came upon them through the diligence of Ohsugi's grandson. And as you likely now realize, The Belgian's recent departure included a large shipment of these items, packed as the shunga have been – to avoid easy detection by Customs' officials, with bribes to be paid along the way."

"I see." And almost as an afterthought Hamish added, "Why did you call these women in the photographs common street prostitutes? Aren't they *geisha*?"

"Geisha? What do you know of geisha, Hamish-san?"

Hamish's face was now as red as it had ever been. After a long pause, he responded to Toshiro's question.

"Awhile back, Kashiwara told me he was mighty pleased with my contribution to his workshop's success and arranged a geisha visit for me, in appreciation."

Toshiro pondered this news for a bit and then asked, "Hamish-san, please give me a description of your encounter with *her*. You need not go into great detail, if doing so will make you uncomfortable."

Hamish stammered a bit, uncertain as to what information Toshiro desired. Then the samurai broke the silence.

"For example, how did you travel to the geisha house? Do you recall where it was located?"

"Geisha house? She came to *my* quarters – Kashiwara's guesthouse."

"She did? How did she arrive?"

"By jinrikisha – and the runner waited for her until she was ready to leave."

"How long did she stay?"

Now Hamish was truly unsettled. He assumed the brevity of the woman's visit would reflect negatively upon his manly prowess. But at this point, he felt compelled to be honest with his new-found friend.

"She was only there about twenty minutes, Toshiro-san."

"Twenty minutes? It is very important that you let go of your obvious embarrassment, Hamish-san, and briefly describe the encounter."

Hamish took a deep breath. "She came into the guesthouse, danced around for a few minutes and then went straightaway to my sleeping pallet. I

followed her and found her lying there, already.....
undressed. It was all over quickly – I have been away
from San Francisco so long, you know – and missed
the ladies back there, so it was .....quick- like."

Toshiro and Hiro exchanged glances again and
then Toshiro spoke.

"My friend, that woman was not *geisha* – but a
common prostitute of the streets. Kashiwara is not
the type of employer to reward anyone with such an
expensive gift as a geisha session. She may even be
one of the women in these photographs."

Hamish glanced at the pictures again, but was
uncertain regarding the matter. He dared not verbalize that he had not yet learned to readily distinguish all Japanese persons from one another, although he did not subscribe to the oft-heard view among Western tourists – *they all look alike!*

When Hamish offered nothing else, Toshiro told
him, "Upon your next visit, I shall instruct you on
the history and practice of geisha and you will understand my certainty regarding the status of the woman
who visited you."

All that Hamish could offer at this time, in his still-disoriented state of mind was, "Thank you, Toshiro-san."

After more consumption of sake, Toshiro spoke
again.

"Forgive me, Hamish-san, but I must raise a delicate issue. I would be an ungracious host and disloyal
friend if I did not warn you of the danger in which
Kashiwara placed you by exposing you to a woman
of the streets. May I have Hiro write an address
for you, so you may direct a jinrikisha runner to a
respected practitioner of ancient medical arts. He is
an old man, but very skilled in both diagnosis and

treatment. He served many samurai in the past and will examine you for evidence of .....*pollution*.

Hiro will also prepare another note describing why you have come to him. He will likely prescribe a *miraculous* ointment for you to apply, and a secret mixture of tea and herbs for you to drink. I would be much relieved if you would allow me to make this referral for you."

Hamish now began to perspire, wondering *what* Kashiwara's *geisha* might have infected him with during their brief mechanical encounter. Back home, he routinely washed his genitals with a solution sold under-the-counter at a tobacconist's shop – after each visit to the Morton Street bordello. Now, the thought of contracting a possibly-exotic disease in Japan was a stressful vexation – so it made sense to accept Toshiro's offer of concern and assistance.

"It's mighty kind of you to give me that information, Toshiro-san."

When they parted later, Toshiro warned Hamish to avoid letting Kashiwara ever know of his discovery regarding why he *really* was brought to this strange land to teach his modern skill to the workshop's staff. Hamish solemnly agreed, but during his remaining weeks in Japan, he would have to struggle to appear naïve around Kashiwara. He was angry, having been gulled into thinking his employer hired him for legal, honest work. Now, he almost felt *unclean*, which was ironic since it had already occurred to him that the Japanese people were the cleanest, most hygienic race he had ever encountered. Without a doubt, however, he would never look again at his *Purinsu* in the same initially-favorable light.

At his first opportunity he stole away to the old herbalist's quarters and presented the note Hiro prepared, describing his problem. The smiling, bowing old gentleman gestured for Hamish to unbutton his trousers, and then used a pair of common wooden chopsticks to lift and move his penis about for examination, and then to part and lift his testicles for the same purpose.

When he was through, as Toshiro had predicted, he handed Hamish a jar of ointment and pantomimed spreading it on his genitals. He also handed him a packet of tea powder mixed with pungent, foul-smelling herbs. He held up a single finger, which Hamish understood to mean *drink one cup of tea each day*.

Over the next few days, Hamish frequently examined his genitals and thought obsessively about his health, but by the time he arrived for his next visit with Toshiro, he was confident he had suffered no ill-effects from his brief encounter with Kashiwara's *gift*.

He was aware, however, that the process of outwardly tolerating Kashiwara in the future would be much more stressful and difficult than ever. As a result of this consequent alienation from his employer and loss of enthusiasm for his work, he was increasingly drawn under the influence of Toshiro, in whom he invested great trust, respect and awe.

SEVENTEEN

Mr. Ohsugi greeted Hamish at the villa's gate and led him through the courtyard garden, upon his next visit. Toshiro and Hiro were waiting for him on the narrow porch, and bowed as he ascended the steps. Hamish returned this fundamental gesture of Japanese etiquette, removed his shoes and entered the house.

At the same time that he noticed his hosts were wearing identical white kimono-style robes, Toshiro gestured toward the garments and spoke.

"We are wearing *yukata* today – most appropriate for the day's events. There is one for you behind the folding screen. Would you be so kind as to remove your clothing and cover yourself with the robe?"

Hamish hesitated for a moment – puzzled, his conundrum obvious to Toshiro who spoke again, with a smile.

"All will be revealed, friend, in due time."

Now somewhat relaxed and trusting, Hamish walked behind the screen and hung his clothing on a nearby wall peg. When he put on the yukata he was impressed by how lightweight and comfortable it felt – apparently made of the softest cotton.

He emerged from behind the screen to find Hiro arranging two flowers in a vase, with a bit of greenery. Toshiro was kneeling nearby and gestured for Hamish to join them.

"We shall have *tea* today, prepared by Hiro. It is more appropriate for today's discussion."

Hamish watched Hiro exert as much care in performing the flower arranging and the tea ceremony as had the samurai during his initial visit. After the tea cup had been passed around several times, Toshiro broke the silence.

"May I inquire as to whether you visited the herbalist, as I suggested, Hamish-san?"

Hamish cleared his throat and answered, "Yes, Toshiro-san."

"And were you pleased with the encounter?"

"He gave me ointment and tea, as you reckoned he would."

"Good! That means he found nothing worrisome when he examined you. He did examine you closely, did he not?"

"Yes, Sir."

"And so, I expect you will be fine – he is very competent."

Then Toshiro turned the conversation elsewhere.

"You are here today to learn of geisha, Hamish-san. There is great misunderstanding among foreign visitors to our land regarding this ancient, noble profession. Like you, most Westerners believe geisha are common prostitutes. But they are *not*. When you leave here today I hope you will be convinced that Kashiwara's *gift* was but a common prostitute, not a geisha."

Hamish nodded, indicating he was eager to be enlightened, and was immediately startled by Toshiro's next pronouncement.

"Geisha were originally only *males*, variously called *taikomuchi* or *houkan*."

This statement elicited the desired effect, as

• The Meiji Prince •

Hamish bolted upright from his slouched, cross-legged position and leaned forward, anxious to learn more.

"Starting in the 13th century, the feudal lords of old Japan, the *Daimyo*, were served by attendants who told humorous stories, sang songs, danced and performed other entertainments for their masters. I believe in Europe, kings had similar attendants known as *court jesters*. In Japan these attendants also prepared and served the Daimyo's tea – as did Hiro today, and were often allowed the privilege of advising their masters regarding military strategy. Some even joined them in battle."

Since Hamish was obviously following this discussion with rapt attention, Toshiro happily continued.

"During the 15th century, widespread peace led to these persons becoming solely *entertainers*, and as such they acquired the title, *geisha – person of the arts*. Thus, one patronized them to be entertained by their mastery of traditional Japanese arts. However, by the 17th century, *women* came to dominate the profession. Under the Tokugawa Shogunate the Port of Nagasaki was opened to Portuguese and Chinese traders seeking entertainment and relaxation from the stress of their labors, and a session with a geisha was much sought after. This coincided with the time when women were at last allowed to appear in female roles on the stage – roles previously reserved for men. As a result, in increasing numbers women entered the arts and entertainment – as geisha. And today, they dominate. The rise of the merchant class, through increased foreign trade, also resulted in many wealthy local residents who were in a position to spend lavishly on such services."

Hamish attempted to absorb this fascinating information.

"Are *all* geisha now women?"

"No, Hamish-san, a few are men, but most are women. As young girls, they are attached to a geisha house where they undergo many years of rigorous training in the arts, entertainment, and intelligent conversation. They are promoted through various ranks until they qualify as full-fledged geisha," and then turning toward Hiro, Toshiro added, "Their training is no less *disciplined* than that of a samurai page – except it lacks the military aspect and the dangers of the battlefield."

"I see," Hamish replied. "This is mighty interesting, Toshiro-san, but why are entertainers confused with prostitutes?"

"Sometimes, depending upon the state of mind and the desire of the client, there may be an intimate encounter during the geisha session. It is usually something which develops as time passes and the skilled geisha is able to assess the client's needs. Japan is now filled with merchants and workers in the rapidly-spreading commercial trades. These men do not live by traditional Japanese religious and philosophical values – something we ought to discuss during your *next* visit. Instead, they live solely for the accumulation of wealth. They are tense and anxious much of the time, obsessed with financial gain. Thus, they walk through the beautiful gardens surrounding their lavish villas and obtain no solace from the respite and peace nature has to offer them. It is the task and duty of the skilled geisha to assess the client's needs and seek to fulfill them. Sometimes, that may include sexual intimacy and release of one kind or another. Surely you now understand that

Kashiwara's gift was not a geisha, merely a common prostitute."

"Yes, Toshiro-san," Hamish mumbled.

And then, Toshiro turned in Hiro's direction and said something to him in Japanese, before returning to address Hamish.

"Hiro has agreed to briefly illustrate the manner in which you would have been treated by your visitor, if she had been a true geisha."

"Hiro is going to do this?" Hamish exclaimed, his surprise most evident.

Toshiro smiled, "Remember, geisha were originally *men*, and some do still practice this honorable, ancient profession. And also remember what I told you during your first visit here – that we believe all creatures are composed of a blending of the yin and the yang. Since samurai training involves activities embracing *both* qualities, Hiro is well-prepared to entertain you today. In fact, he has already begun the session by bowing to you when you arrived, providing a comfortable garment for you to wear while here today, preparing a beautiful flower arrangement for you to contemplate – and preparing a relaxing tea. Now, he wishes to entertain you further. Are you receptive?"

Hamish blushed in embarrassment, feeling he had appeared rude, and quickly replied, "Yes, Yes, Sir. I'd be mighty honored."

After a few more Japanese words were exchanged between Toshiro and Hiro, the young Page rose and appeared to *glide* across the floor in a delicate movement, which took him to a cabinet from which he removed a small drum. He then knelt beside Hamish and began to beat upon it with wooden sticks. Toshiro pointed to the drum and identified it as *kodaiko*.

Soon, Hiro replaced the drum with an even

smaller one which he mounted on his right shoulder and tapped with the fingers of his left hand, while he danced quite sensually, around the room. Toshiro pointed to the second drum, *sutsumi*.

Hamish found himself quite stimulated by the erotic movements of the usually-reserved Hiro. And then the young Page reached behind a cabinet and retrieved a stringed instrument. At first, Hamish mistook it for an American banjo. Hiro knelt beside him and began to strike the three strings with a small wooden spatula. Toshiro then pointed to the instrument and identified it as *shamisen*. Shortly, Hiro started to sing in a high-pitched voice, as he played. Hamish had no idea of the meaning of the Japanese words – but if he had, he may have been embarrassed by the lyrics, which spoke of the undying love between male comrades.

Hiro next played a bamboo flute. Once again, Toshiro identified it with a single word, *shakuhachi*. The music was very sensual, and the way Hiro caressed the flute as he played added to Hamish's increasing absorption in the moment. Happily, for his level of comfort, he did not know that *shakuhachi* was common Japanese slang for *fellatio*.

After Hiro eventually put down the flute, he said something in his native tongue to Toshiro, and Toshiro interpreted for Hamish.

"Hiro senses you are very tense and stressed today. Is that so, Hamish-san?"

With a delayed deep sigh, Hamish responded.

"The news that Kashiwara has turned my art into a dirty business is mighty vexatious. I was first gulled into believing he was someone he wasn't, and I was also hired for a very different reason than I reckoned.

It has gnawed at me. My father taught me as a lad to treat people different than that."

"You father must have been an honorable man, Hamish-san. But while your disappointment in Kashiwara can never be fully dissipated – and you *must* keep it hidden from him, Hiro may be able to assist you in releasing some of your frustration. After all, that is what a caring geisha would do in this situation."

Hamish threw a sharp glance at Hiro, and then one back at Toshiro. *What is Toshiro suggesting?* He wondered.

Toshiro could read the confusion on his guest's face and quickly added, "Hiro has suggested a *massage* may be of value at this time."

"A massage – well, yes. I never did have one, but I've seen places in San Francisco that offer them."

Toshiro said something to Hiro, who left the room briefly and returned with a small, rolled-up pallet. He unrolled it, placed it on the tatami, and motioned Hamish in its direction.

"Lie face-down on the pallet, Hamish-san," Toshiro directed, "and let Hiro's skillful, soothing hands assist you. I, myself, am familiar with their healing power."

Hamish did as he was told and was soon straddled by Hiro. The Page massaged his neck, shoulders, upper arms, back, legs – and even his buttocks, all while Hamish continued to wear the yukata robe. The physical pleasure Hamish felt was only exceeded by the excitement of having this beautiful young man caressing – *possessing* him in such an intimate manner. And all the while, Hamish was aware that Toshiro watched, intensely focused on the scene. Hamish could not feel Hiro's member swelling as their bodies pressed against one another, but he was aware that he was now fully erect.

After a time, Hiro stopped, stood up and bowed deeply at Hamish.

"Aha," Toshiro exclaimed, "your geisha session has come to an end. Now do you see clearly that woman of Kashiwara's was not geisha?"

As Hamish struggled to his feet, well-aware his erection pressed visibly against the thin robe, he responded, "Oh, yes, Toshiro-san. Thank you and Hiro." Then, turning to the Page he bowed deeply – more deeply than protocol required, and returned to his cross-legged position on the tatami.

"And now," Toshiro announced, "one final introduction to our customs today – the Japanese ritual of the *bath*. Now you can understand why we have worn these robes during your visit."

Hamish was again surprised, and immediately thought of the public baths in San Francisco, which he occasionally visited for a good cleansing that was more thorough than the usual sponge-bath in his small living quarters. Those baths were dark, dank, foul-smelling places filled with filthy gold prospectors briefly in town from the fields to replenish their supplies, or dock workers, ships' crews newly arrived from long voyages, and the like. Such visits were always unsettling experiences for him. Thus, he was uncertain as to how to conduct himself in the present situation. However, the ever-vigilant, perceptive Toshiro came to his aid.

"In Japan, Hamish-san, one does not enter the bath for the purpose of *cleansing* oneself."

Hamish's facial response reflected his confusion, and Toshiro continued.

"One cleanses oneself *before* entering the bath.

• The Meiji Prince •

Thus, the bath is primarily a place to relax, to be soothed. In your case, today it will be to relieve any residual stress after Hiro's artful geisha session."

Hamish smiled, relieved.

"Come," Toshiro said, as he rose from the tatami. Hiro and Hamish then followed him to a small room at the back of the villa. Several low wooden stools and wooden buckets were placed on the tiled floor – which had a drain hole. White towels hung on wall-pegs, and a square wood-encased tub filled with water was in a corner.

"Our custom is to wrap one's towel around one's head until it is time to dry off. You may use the towel peg to hang your robe upon, in the meantime."

Toshiro and Hiro quickly performed these actions, and only afterward did Hamish reluctantly do the same – aware that his erection had only partially subsided. However, there was nothing he could do to alter the situation or hide it, under the present circumstances. Then, after Toshiro and Hiro both sat on the wooden stools, Hamish followed. Almost immediately, Mr. Ohsugi appeared and filled the small buckets near their stools with water from a larger bucket he brought into the room. After he did so, he handed soap to Toshiro.

"Our guest shall be first," Toshiro exclaimed, while handing the soap to Hamish. Hamish dipped it into the bucket and began to lather his upper body. After he was well-lathered, he handed the soap to Toshiro, who later passed it on to Hiro. Then, Mr. Ohsugi poured water over each of them, in turn. While Ohsugi went for more water – Hamish assumed there was a fresh spring at the back of the villa, Toshiro and Hiro stood up and the soap was once again handed to Hamish. It occurred to their American guest that it was time to lather his lower body. He stood and did so, trying to ignore his semi-erect member. His embarrassment was enhanced by the fact that neither Toshiro nor Hiro was in a priapic state. However, his stolen glances in their direction revealed each was of more modest endowment than he, which raised his spirits a bit.

After all three had lathered their lower extremities, Mr. Ohsugi returned with more rinsing water to pour over them. When they had all been thoroughly rinsed, Toshiro spoke.

"Now we may enter the bathing tub."

Hamish was directed to enter first, followed by Toshiro and then Hiro. They sat in the tub, saying very little, obviously enjoying the sensual pleasure of the water caressing their naked bodies. It struck Hamish that he had rarely felt so relaxed in his entire life. He also was aware that he had never before experienced the level of intimacy and comradeship with other men that he did at this moment, in the presence of Toshiro and Hiro.

EIGHTEEN

After Hamish returned to Kashiwara's villa from his orientation to the history of the geisha at Toshiro's home, he realized his employer might routinely inquire as to their latest topic of conversation. However, he knew he could *not* tell him the truth, for then Kashiwara would realize that Hamish was aware he had been treated by his employer to a common prostitute and not a professional geisha. He therefore decided to simply tell him the samurai desired to learn about life in California.

There was no need, however, for the subterfuge, as Kashiwara made no such inquiry. At this stage in Hamish's relationship with Toshiro, Kashiwara had become convinced it was unlikely that a portrait commission from the famous former samurai would be forthcoming. And despite the disappointment that thought brought him, he was consoled by the benefits he had already reaped from the relationship between the two.

For Kashiwara had continued to spread the word that his American employee was now a trusted member of Toshiro's inner circle – and as a result, the merchant class in Tokyo flocked to his workshop to purchase his merchandise. Many also insisted Hamish personally photograph them in his studio at the villa – the cachet of having been photographed by Toshiro's *friend* was a subject for boasting. By the same token, the foreign traders who came into contact with Kashiwara did so largely because they believed he was a *Prince*. Whether native or foreign, the increasingly-wealthy merchant class reveled in such social *connections*. In the case of the locals, the prestige came from a tenuous connection to a renowned retired samurai, and for the foreigners it was their involvement with an ersatz Prince. In either case, as a result, Kashiwara's financial gains from the friendship between Hamish and Toshiro mounted, and he therefore had no desire to interfere with their relationship.

Upon the next visit, Toshiro followed through with his suggestion that they discuss Japan's religious and philosophical traditions. He reiterated to Hamish that the Westernization of Japan was leading to their diminution in importance among the burgeoning merchant class, whose materialistic goals left little room for such old-fashioned *distractions*.

"I believe we should begin with a discussion of Shintoism, Hamish-san, for it is the indigenous religion of Japan and now the official state religion under the Emperor Meiji."

Hamish nodded in agreement, as he accepted the cup of tea being passed among the three of them following Hiro's having conducted the tea ceremony.

"But first, I believe it is now appropriate for me to think of you as my *Gakusei* – my student, and for you to view me as your *Sensei* – teacher. Is that acceptable to you, Hamish-san?"

Hamish only hesitated for a moment before replying, "Yes, Sensei." He could not have been more flattered than to know this famous samurai had not only befriended him for some weeks now, but was elevating him to such a treasured position.

Toshiro smiled and continued.

"Shintoism is a *nature* religion that has roots in ancient China. Various gods of nature are worshipped – such as the mountain god, river god, sun god, rice-paddy god, rock god. Ultimately there are dozens of Shinto gods, but the faithful do not worship icons representing them. The focus instead is on *animism* – the belief that natural phenomena and objects are alive and have souls. Thus, spirits are seen to reside in all objects. Also, Shintoists do not believe in heaven or hell, but accept a form of afterlife. Have you visited any of their shrines while here, Gakusei?"

"Yes, Sensei, I photographed several after coming upon them while driving my darkroom cart around the City, looking for possible postcard subjects."

"And what do you recall of them?"

"They always seem to have a bright red wooden gate. And often there are stacks of sake barrels at the entrance."

"Those are offerings to the sake god. You likely saw stone or metal lanterns at the entrance as well – donated by the public as memorials to their ancestors. What did you notice of the behavior of Japanese worshippers who visited the shrines?"

"I saw them washing their hands and then clapping them, but it was all mighty confusing."

"They were preparing to pray. They must wash their hands before they enter the gate, after which they approach a long wooden box in front of the shrine and bow twice. They then clap their hands to attract the gods' attention, and make a prayerful wish. Coins are thrown into the wooden box as an offering to the gods so wishes will be granted."

"I see, Sensei. As I wandered around I felt a mite like I was at one of the street fairs in San Francisco."

"How so?"

"Well, vendors were selling small items of wood and trinkets, and many people were buying them."

"You are speaking of the wooden *votive* tablets which may be purchased in blank form – allowing the supplicant to write a personal wish, or with standard wishes already inscribed."

"Wishes – for what, Sensei?"

"For good health, a happy marriage, wealth, a male child. You likely also saw talismans sold, which are believed to aid in the fulfillment of these wishes. Shintoism is actually a rather simple religion, with no elaborate rituals. Its primary goal is to keep humans and nature in harmony. This religious philosophy has secular benefits, as it helps foster a sense of *community* at the local level in Japan."

"So folks will act neighborly and respectful?"

"One could say that, Gakusei. The emphasis is upon the human-nature relationship, rather than elaborate rituals, a priestly hierarchy, or a sacred text. The simple rituals conducted by Shinto priests focus upon making the various gods feel respected and well-served by worshippers, so they will continue to bring good fortune in the future. One insures this through prayer, supplication and offerings of food, coins."

"I did have a right-peaceful feeling when I walked around the shrines and their gardens, Sensei."

"For Westerners steeped in religions which focus upon guilt, Shintoism can offer great solace – for it views human bodily functions, including the *sexual* ones, as normal and necessary for a healthy physical, mental, and spiritual life."

Hamish had never heard preachers back home

discuss sexual functions as anything other than great temptations for evil-doing, occasions for guilt and sin in the eyes of the Christian god. Therefore, he found Toshiro's comments on the Shinto view especially interesting.

After the tea cup was passed several more times, Toshiro continued.

"Of course the teachings of Confucius also came to us from China – particularly in the form of his *Analects*, which promoted ancestor worship, filial piety, and love of order in government – all of which have found a welcome home here. However, unlike the prominent *religions*, his philosophy is not concentrated in temples, shrines, or churches and is therefore less visible and less relevant to today's discussion. The influence of Buddha and his adherents in Japan is an entirely different matter."

"I see many Buddhist temples about the town, decorated with statues – mighty different from the simple Shinto shrines."

"Yes, and let me add to your observations, Gakusei. Buddhism traveled from India to China, then to Korea, and finally to Japan in the 6th century. It is a view that the world around us is illusory, transitory. It teaches that one must transcend this world through great mental discipline which will lead to ultimate *enlightenment*. One begins by sitting in the *lotus* position and applying mental exercises which are learned through years of study and practice."

"I've seen many statues of Buddha sitting in the same way, in all of them. Is that the lotus?"

"Yes it is. Now there are four cardinal virtues in Buddhism: compassion, renunciation, equality and nonviolence. To achieve and practice them, one contemplates the many icons in the temples, chants and prays. The ultimate key to salvation is to *know yourself*. Do you know yourself, Gakusei?"

Hamish wasn't expecting to be questioned by Toshiro on this day – he expected only to listen to an exposition on the local religions. Startled, he did not respond.

"I ask again, Hamish-san, do you know yourself?"

Stammering, Hamish muttered, "I reckon so.....I mean, I knew it was time to leave my routine life back home and have an adventure far away."

"That is commendable, but rather superficial. Do you *really* know yourself as the Buddhists advocate?"

Forlornly, and realizing he would not be able to satisfy his Sensei on the matter, Hamish sighed, "I reckon not."

Toshiro smiled benevolently and continued.

"Buddhism believes there is hope for all who are willing to follow the path to enlightenment. But it is proving to be especially difficult for Westerners, because they are not prone to self-reflection or self-discipline in their approach to life, to the world. There is a sect of Buddhism – *Zen*, which emphasizes silence, meditation and control of the mind and self in the extreme. I doubt it will ever take hold in your part of the world."

Hamish nodded, mechanically, realizing he had nothing of consequence to add to the discussion at this point.

"Unlike Shintoism, Buddhists believe in heaven and hell. They also emphasize ancestor worship, which is popular here."

"Begging your pardon, Sensei – you said a bit ago that Shintoism is the official state religion of Japan. Where does that leave Buddhism?"

"An excellent question, Gakusei! One interesting

aspect regarding the study of religion is that one finds it often intertwined with politics. For example, Buddhism was favored and protected under the Tokugawa Shogunate. The resulting alliance led many Buddhist monks to side with the outgoing Tokugawa in their struggle with the forces which led to the Meiji Restoration. And so now, as punishment for what the monks saw as loyalty to their Tokugawa protectors – but the Meiji viewed as disloyalty to the Emperor, much Buddhist property possessed by the rebel monks has been confiscated. Some temples have been closed forcibly, and many icons and other temple treasures have *disappeared*."

"The monks must have been mighty peeved. Did they fight back?"

"Hamish-san, they are *pacifists*."

Before Hamish could respond, Toshiro signaled to Hiro that he wanted more tea, and the cup was passed around several more times before he spoke again.

"Now it is time to mention *your* people, the Christians. I assume you are Christian, Hamish-san?"

"Yes – I was baptized and attended Sunday school when I was younger. But I'm not a regular churchgoer now, Sensei."

"The Christian creed found its way here, but with mixed results. It all began when Jesuit missionaries from Portugal arrived three centuries ago and initially made themselves useful as translators for Western travelers. Soon, more-aggressive Spanish Jesuits followed and before long their focus was entirely upon converting my people from what they viewed as *heathenism, paganism*. As a result, the Japanese found them arrogant in their refusal to understand, appreciate and respect the religious traditions already in place. Their offensive behavior became so intolerable that they were expelled from our land in 1562. But they gradually returned by making inroads at various ports and towns under the direct control of local chieftains who could be bribed. But their pernicious behavior continued and eventually led to the Tokugawa expelling all foreign priests from the land."

"But I've seen some Christian churches in my travels around Tokyo, Sensei."

"Yes – under the Meiji Government they are tolerated again, provided they do not preach against our belief that the Emperor is *God*."

Hamish was puzzled. "That must be mighty hard for them to do – Christians believe there is only Jesus the Christ."

"Yes, but once again, politics enters religious discourse. The Meiji are willing to tolerate Christianity upon the condition I just mentioned, and the Christians are willing to accept *that* compromise in order to gain local converts. In the middle of it all are the ambitious Japanese merchants and traders who are becoming Christian in order to better their opportunities for Western trade. These people have convinced members of the Court that such alliances can only benefit Japan's rapid march toward modernization. And so, the accommodation had been reached – for now. Who knows what tomorrow may bring, in a society no longer enjoying the stability and traditions of its glorious past?"

Now, a noticeable glaze seemed to appear over Toshiro's eyes and Hamish felt his Sensei was no longer present in the room. At the same time, Hiro looked downward, saying nothing and not moving – so Hamish did the same. After a time, Toshiro spoke again, apparently *back* from the mysterious place to which he had gone.

"I hope, Hamish-san, I have been helpful today in clarifying the religious confusion you have been encountering here. What is it you wish me to discuss upon your next visit?"

Hamish pretended to ponder the question, knowing full well he had been struggling to hold back that which preyed on his mind for some time. After what he concluded to be a thoughtful interval, he spoke.

"I reckon I'd like to know more about the *samurai*, Sensei."

Toshiro smiled.

"And so you shall, Hamish-san. And so you shall."

NINETEEN

"I thought we would have sake, rather than tea, today," Toshiro said, after he and Hamish were seated. "It is more appropriate for today's discussion – since it is the favored drink of the samurai, of whom you wish to know more."

Hamish smiled, just as Hiro entered the room with the sake decanter and cups on a tray. After all had been served, Hiro sat on the tatami near Toshiro, and everyone drank until the Master began his recitation.

"The noble, hereditary, ancient profession of the samurai was meant *to serve*. A samurai is *one who serves*. At the highest level, they served the Shogun. Lower were those who served the daimyo, provincial lords who in turn served the Shogun. When a samurai lost his Lord, due to death or political maneuvering, he became a *ronin* – destined to wander the land seeking employment as a paid mercenary. *My* family has always served the Shogun directly, and as a result a modest estate accumulated – some of which you now see around you."

Hamish nodded, indicating he was listening intently.

"Despite their reputation as fierce warriors, they also cultivated the arts – particularly poetry, painting and gardening, in keeping with the presence of the yin and the yang in the temperament of all persons. The samurai lived by a strict code of conduct, adhering to seven principles: duty and loyalty; justice and morality; sincerity; public courtesy; compassion; heroic courage; and honor."

"That's a right-strict code, Sensei."

'Yes, Gakusei, and a complex one. These principles were derived over time from a number of sources – Confucianism, Taoism, Shintoism, Buddhism. Following these codes, the samurai served this nation, its rulers, and its people – for centuries. We even had our own local currency – *hansatu*. But then, following the overthrow of the Tokugawa Shogunate, everything changed – for the Meiji Government viewed us as reactionaries and painful reminders of Japan's feudal, isolated past. And as this nation rushed to join the modern West, we were stripped of our rights, one-by-one."

"Your rights, Sensei?"

"Yes, Gakusei. A samurai's sword is his *soul*, and yet we were ordered to surrender ours to the authorities – both the long and the short one. These were spiritual objects to us, passed down through generations. I only retain mine because I made a solemn personal pledge to the Emperor to never take them beyond the walls of my villa. But that is a rare exception, granted only because of my family's long and esteemed history. Also, our elaborate warrior uniforms can no longer be worn. And we further suffered the great indignity of having to cut off our highly-symbolic topknots. These dictates were humiliating and aimed at destroying our noble profession, which thrived for hundreds of years."

"Where are the samurai now, Sensei? Do they all live quietly, like you?"

Toshiro frowned. "You have seen them among the

old men who beg in the streets. Many among those beggars are former samurai who served less-powerful daimyo, or were wandering ronin who lost their masters. There are also many hiding in the forests and the mountainsides, talking of a rebellion to come against the Government. However, to do so *now* is to also rebel against the Emperor – the most disloyal and unforgivable of acts, for he is *God*. Only a few former samurai live in modest comfort such as I do."

"I reckon they are dying out, then. Will they be forgotten in years to come?"

"Never! Never, Gakusei! Much has been recorded of the samurai in song, poetry, literature and art – which will live on. Let me offer you an example. Have you heard *The Tale of the Forty-Seven Ronin?*"

"No, Sensei."

"I can assure you, Gakusei, it is a tale which will last forever – it has already traveled from the written scroll to paintings and woodcuts, to the Kabuki stage and the Bunraku puppet world. But let me enlighten you. The forty-seven ronin were originally samurai who served a daimyo, Lord Asano. Their Lord was repeatedly insulted by the Shogun's chief household manager at Edo Castle – Lord Kira. One day, Lord Asano could no longer tolerate this disrespect and so he slashed Lord Kira with his short sword. Although Lord Kira survived, the Shogun was horrified by this attempt to kill Lord Kira and ordered Lord Asano to commit *seppuku*, so he could die with honor."

"Seppuku?"

"Seppuku is ritual suicide, committed to retain one's honor. When a criminal commits seppuku, his estate remains intact for his heirs. If he doesn't, and has to be put to death by others, his estate is confiscated and often given to the aggrieved party. But continuing with the tale – after Lord Asano ended his life in this honorable manner, his loyal samurai became wandering ronin, having no master to lead them anymore. After several years, they avenged their master by going to Lord Kira's home and beheading him. They then took his head to Lord Asano's grave. Several months later, they all committed seppuku together, as it was the only honorable thing they could do under the circumstances. And their story will live *forever*, in one form or another."

Hamish thought for awhile, drinking sake in order to give himself time to collect his thoughts before speaking.

"To Christians, suicide is a *sin* – a terrible sin."

"Yes – but for us, seppuku is an act of *supreme sincerity*."

Hamish said nothing further, but continued to sip the sake which Hiro kept flowing by frequently leaving the room to refill the decanter. After a time, Toshiro continued.

"There is one other area of which I must speak, in order to give you a full understanding of the samurai way. However, it is a rather delicate one for someone with your Christian scruples."

Toshiro's words caused Hamish to straighten his back and become especially alert, in order to capture what would follow.

"I speak of *love*, in all its forms. In your world, only the love of a man for a woman is celebrated. But here, our ancient traditions teach us that *love is love, all love is equal*."

As Toshiro anticipated, Hamish now began to shift nervously in his cross-legged sitting position.

"Among the samurai, it is honorable to love women *and* men, or *only* men."

Hamish could feel the slow, hot flush spreading across his face, and he automatically wiped his right cheek with his hand – as if to somehow erase the growing scarlet stain by so doing. However, Toshiro was not surprised by Hamish's reaction.

"You will recall we talked earlier of the influence of Buddhism in Japan. Among the monks and priests who developed a codified temple culture, sex with women was proscribed. It was therefore only natural that the monks and priests would seek an outlet by transferring their desires to *chigo* – their acolytes at the monastery. A body of literature eventually evolved, *Chigo Monogatori* – The Acolyte Tales. It was then only a matter of time before the samurai would adopt this philosophy."

Hamish struggled to speak, and when he finally could, he asked, "Are there acolytes in the samurai world too?"

Toshiro laughed. "No, but we have *pages* with whom such relations are known as *wakashu*."

Hearing that, Hamish looked in Hiro's direction. Ordinarily, during his discussions with Toshiro, Hiro sat by the latter's side and stared at the tatami. He said very little but was quick to respond to any of his Master's requests. Now, however, Hiro turned toward Hamish and directly looked into his eyes. Hiro neither blinked nor moved, and soon Hamish was the one to first look away. The moment was not lost on Toshiro.

"Our literature is filled with male-male love themes from as far back as the Heian Period in the 8th century. Such love is called *nanshoku*. One of the greatest literary works in Japanese literature is The Great Mirror of Male Love – *Nanshoku Okagani*, which the Meiji Government is now trying to suppress. All they are doing is driving it underground, where it will continue to be enjoyed by traditionalists."

Toshiro drank more sake, deliberately allowing Hamish time to absorb what he had said. When his student's face appeared to be less flushed, he continued.

"Such love is time-honored and has inspired much art. As far back as the 8th century the Heian Court bestowed the honorific title of *Kobo Daishi* upon the mystic Buddhist teacher, Kukai, who argued that the love of men is an essential part of the artistic process. There is a fine example of this position in the life of Zeami, who in the 14th century founded the theatrical form, *Noh* – believing it to be a spiritual art form for male actors, and which later became much admired by samurai. Zeami loved men, although he was also married to a woman. In poetry, Basho, whose birth name was Matsuo Munefusa, created many beautiful haiku verses in the 17th century, extolling intimate male comradeship. Actually, there was an explosion of such poetry in the 17th century, as many older men composed poems on the theme of love directed toward younger companions. Such pursuits were called *wakashud* – the way of youth. While these developments were occurring in the arts, Buddhist thought among the most-highly educated, upper-class samurai led to the long-held view that love between men is superior to that between men and women."

Toshiro perceived Hamish's discomfort and confusion – obvious from his fidgeting, and recognized he was struggling with this information and therefore needed time to absorb it.

"Perhaps we should end our discussion of the samurai here, Gakusei. But first, I wish to make one more point so you may more-fully appreciate the precarious position into which we have been placed under the Meiji Government. The British gentleman – Darwin, have you heard of him?"

Hamish shook his head from side-to-side.

"My British tutor discussed him and his writing when he taught me English. Darwin argued that *strength* plus *adaptation* lead to *survival*. Samurai surely have strength, but are we willing to adapt to the new Regime and its rush toward Western modernization? You may have noted that there are no *frogs* in my garden. As soon as one is discovered there, it is quickly removed. Frogs are the symbol of *change* in Japan and therefore are not welcome guests *here*. However, Darwin warns all – including the samurai, that adaptation is necessary for survival, and not strength alone. At this point in my nation's history, there is little indication samurai wish to adapt to the modern world – surely not among those massing in forests and upon mountainsides, threatening rebellion. And so, you may one day reflect when back in California that you were present at the *sunset* of the noble, glorious institution of the samurai."

Hamish nodded, but before he could say, *Thank you, Sensei – it was all mighty interesting*, Toshiro spoke once more.

"Next time you come, Hiro and I will take you on a little journey. You will have the chance to see something you will never see in San Francisco, I am sure!"

TWENTY

As soon as Mr. Ohsugi opened the gate for Hamish upon his next visit to Toshiro's villa, the anxious guest rushed to the villa's porch – where he found Toshiro and Hiro waiting for him. After bows were exchanged, Toshiro spoke.

"Gakusei, at today's festivities you will better blend in with the others if you dress as we have."

Hamish looked more closely at his comrades' attire, noting they were wearing identical plain, white kimonos.

"Come, I shall assist you," Toshiro beckoned, as he led Hamish indoors and to a folding screen in the corner of the room where they usually sat and drank tea or sake.

"Behind that screen you will find a kimono such as mine. Remove your outer garments – including your footwear and stockings and then I shall assist you with the rest."

Hamish did as he was instructed, filled with anticipation over the promised *mysterious* journey which lay ahead. After he emerged with the kimono loosely hanging from his body, Toshiro approached. He twice-wrapped a piece of cloth around Hamish's waist and then tied it in the back.

"This is an *obi*," Toshiro explained. He then attached a small purse, secured by a miniature ivory carving of a crane – the latter serving as a counterweight to hold the purse in place as it was suspended from the obi sash.

"This little object," he said – pointing to the ivory carving, "is a *netsuke*, and the crane is a symbol of *longevity*, which I wish you. You may now put the valuables you carried here in your trouser pocket into the purse it supports."

Hamish went back to the clothing he had left behind the folding screen, retrieved his money and identification papers, and when he returned Toshiro was holding a pair of stockings and a pair of sandals – both identical to what he wore.

"These stockings are called *tabi*. You will notice they are sewn so the large toe is separated from the others. This allows one to comfortably wear them with these sandals – *setta*. The setta have soles made of leather, but one's feet rest on a surface similar to that of tatami."

After Hamish was duly attired, he and Toshiro joined Hiro and the trio went out a backdoor of the villa and into an alley, where Mr. Ohsugi was found holding the reins of Toshiro's horse – tethered to a hansom cab-like small carriage. Hiro promptly stepped onto the driver's platform at the rear and took the reins from Ohsugi.

"You will ride with me inside, Gakusei," Toshiro said, gesturing toward the passenger seat.

After they were settled, Mr. Ohsugi bowed to the departing little group and the horse led them through a series of streets until Hamish eventually realized they were headed for the surrounding countryside. Occasionally, Toshiro broke the silence, pointing out a scene or object of interest, beauty. After almost two

• The Meiji Prince •

hours Hiro turned the horse and carriage into what appeared to be the courtyard of a small country inn

"Here we shall have lunch before proceeding to our destination – which is nearby. You will see and taste one of our countryside delicacies today, Gakusei."

After they left the carriage, the trio walked behind the inn. Immediately Hamish noted the steam and stench being emitted from a hot pool of bubbling mineral water. A small hut was next to the pool. An attendant wearing a smock, with the symbol of a *black egg* upon it, bowed to the visitors. He then plunged a rack containing fresh white-shelled eggs into the water. After words were exchanged between him and Toshiro, he pulled another rack filled with black-shelled eggs from the bubbling water and offered it to Toshiro.

"You see, Gakusei, this place is known as an *egg house*, and when the eggshells turn black in the hot mineral water, they are hard-cooked and ready to enjoy."

He then nodded to Hiro, who took the rack from the attendant and they returned to the courtyard of the inn, where a server rushed out the door, bowed, and led them to a table and benches under the shade of a tree.

Soon, the eggs were accompanied by sweet rice cakes and sake, and after everyone had had his fill of food and drink – the remaining eggs in the rack were wrapped in thin cloth and stored under the carriage seat, for eating on the way back home.

A short while after their journey resumed, Toshiro broke the silence once more.

"We shall soon be at our destination. I can tell you now that we are going to attend a *harvest* festival."

Hamish instinctively glanced at the surrounding

fields, yet to be shorn of their bounty and replied, "Harvest festival, Sensei – isn't it a mite early for that?"

"Ah – you are quite observant, my friend. Yes, but there is a tactical reason for holding the event *now*. This festival is an honorable ancient ceremony, which the New Government wishes to suppress. It is an embarrassment to them because such an event is not compatible with Japan's rush to Westernization. Government agents and spies will be on alert around the country during harvest-time in several weeks – ready to disrupt such affairs. But by then, we shall have foiled the enemy, under their very noses!"

"I see," Hamish answered excitedly, impressed with the Samurai's cunning.

"In addition," Toshiro continued, "we are holding the event near a small village which has not been associated with the festival in the past. We have also employed utmost discretion in using underground channels to alert participants."

Hamish nodded, conspiratorially. "And what is this festival called, Sensei?"

"It is called *Hadaka Matsuri*."

"I'm graveled about why it is objectionable to the authorities, Sensei. The farming towns surrounding San Francisco all have harvest festivals – and no one gets upset."

Toshiro laughed softly. "Ah, Gakusei, this is like *no* harvest festival in San Francisco, for it is a men's-only affair which celebrates male fertility, as well. I'm sure you understand that the male seed is crucial for the harvest to occur."

Hamish's quizzical facial expression revealed his confusion over Toshiro's statement. Toshiro noted this and added, "Surely you realize no harvest occurs unless the land, the plantings are fertile? But be patient, for we are here now and all will be revealed soon."

Hamish looked up and saw a number of carts, horses, carriages and wagons stationed in a nearby wood – which partially concealed them. As Hiro dismounted, a throng of young boys rushed forward and soon Hamish realized they were seeking a few yen in exchange for feeding, watering and tending to Toshiro's horse and carriage during the festival.

Hiro quickly handled the business regarding the horse and carriage and then the trio began to walk toward a large clearing, surrounded by a thick forest. A number of men, dressed similarly to them, were already milling about at the far end of the clearing. Toshiro pointed to a raised viewing platform at the field's midpoint. "You will observe from there, Gakusei. We shall return to fetch you after the festival."

At that, Toshiro and Hiro bowed to Hamish, he reciprocated, and as they left to join the congregation at the far end of the clearing, he walked toward the spectators' platform. Because he was taller than the adolescent boys and old men who largely populated the viewing stand, he stood at the back. Soon, the crowd Toshiro and Hiro had joined grew to such a size he could no longer easily distinguish them from the others.

Shortly thereafter, a low chanting began among the men and after it became louder, they removed their kimonos and handed them to nearby young boys who collected the garments, carefully. Hamish was startled to see that the men were nearly naked, save for the Japanese loincloth known as a *fundoshi*. He had seen peasant men wearing these garments, while working in rice paddies and at other hard labor – and always found his eyes drawn to the way in which they emphasized the genital area.

And then, a loud blast from a horn caused the spectators to look in the direction of the sound. When they did, Hamish saw six men carrying a litter upon which a wooden box with a large opening at the front was in place. Hamish was immediately reminded of a pet dog's humble backyard quarters.

The litter-bearers brought it to the midpoint of the clearing, directly opposite the spectators' viewing stand. They put it down and then rushed away, as if fearing for their lives. Soon, the crowd of near-naked men formed a large semi-circle around the mysterious object and began to chant in an obviously-taunting manner which even Hamish could understand, despite the language barrier.

After awhile, the head of a large wooden phallus emerged from the opening and a roar went up from the crowd, who leapt backward in exaggerated fear. And then, a totally naked man popped out of the opening and began to chase the others with the phallus. Each time the object touched a *captive*, he immediately stripped off his fundoshi and retreated to the far end of the clearing to await others, in similar straits, to join him there.

The naked man with the phallus rushed among the crowd like a rabid animal, wildly thrusting his hyper-masculine weapon, in an attempt to seize as many of the still-clad taunting creatures as possible.

And as the crowd of now-naked captives on the other end of the clearing grew, they began to gyrate wildly in ways which disturbed and astonished Hamish's sense of public propriety. They shook their torsos so violently that their genitals slapped against their inner thighs. Some boldly thrust their swollen manhood toward each other, and to Hamish's shock – men paired off, with one partner bending over and the other violently simulating penetration of him from behind!

The scene overwhelmed Hamish. His own manhood swelled to its full glory beneath his kimono. He desperately needed relief from the stimulation provided by the unexpected orgiastic scene occurring before him. When all but Toshiro, Hiro and several others were left with their fundoshi intact, the exhausted naked man with the phallus bowed deeply to them and threw down his *weapon* – clearly acknowledging their cunning and stamina in dodging the threat to which the others had succumbed.

At that point, the victors also tore off their fundoshi, and everyone lined up and marched around the clearing several times – singing, chanting, dancing and proudly displaying their genitals, until Hamish's organ erupted involuntarily. Luckily, he had retained his Western undergarments when he donned the kimono and therefore they absorbed the discharge which would have otherwise stained the borrowed garment.

Later – back in the carriage Toshiro, who was soaked with visible perspiration, turned to Hamish and spoke, while Hiro guided the horse on their return to Tokyo.

"Do you not agree, Gakusei, you have never seen such as this on the streets of San Francisco?"

His flush-faced student replied quickly, "Lord Almighty – no, Sensei, not now, not never!"

Toshiro again uttered one of his rare laughs and further elaborated.

"The egg is inert, capable of nothing until the male seed gives it life. This festival pays homage to the power of the male organ, in all its beauty and wonder – and its relation to a bountiful harvest. Those who are captured are weak specimens of manhood – having neither the strength nor cunning to survive. They are therefore stripped of their garments to illustrate their pitiful nakedness in the eyes of others. The few survivors of the ritual, such as Hiro and I, retained our masculinity and inborn power by evading capture. We showed all attending that some men are *superior* and remain true to their birthright – never surrendering to those who would take it from them!"

Hamish struggled to understand all that Toshiro so vigorously and forcefully said to him. "Why did the captured men behave publicly in such a shameful manner after they stripped off their fundoshi?"

"Ah, Gakusei – another excellent question. Weak men also lack self-discipline and willpower over events, which they allow to carry them away with uncontrollable emotional fervor. Once their defeat today had become obvious to all present, their true undisciplined natures emerged. A *true* man chooses the time and place to exhibit his passion – it does not choose him."

Now Hamish was doubly-perplexed. "But Sensei, near the end of the festival, you and Hiro also removed your fundoshi and joined the hurly-burly as the crowd marched around the field – openly...... aroused."

"Yes, Gakusei, but in our case we made a deliberate decision to join in the naked revels – no one else determined that for *us*. Self-discipline and strength, Gakusei – they are what I brought you here to witness today. They are precious gifts of the Samurai gods, and they are bestowed upon but a few worthy individuals."

They rode in silence back to Tokyo, Hamish's head reeling with so much to ponder on this incredible day. By the time they reached the villa, Toshiro indicated he and Hiro were in need of cleansing and a relaxing bath. Hamish was invited to join them – after all Toshiro noted, he was covered with dust from the country roads they traversed, despite the fact he had not actively participated in the festivities.

As they later carried out the elaborate bathing ritual with which Hamish was familiar from a previous visit, he could not completely conceal his still-stubborn partial tumescence. He consoled himself in the belief that his comrades did not notice – *or so he thought*.

As soon as he returned to Kashiwara's guesthouse later that evening, his mind filled with images of gyrating, naked men, he could not help himself – he quickly plunged into the act of self-pleasure, and would repeat this sensuous exercise every evening until he next visited his esteemed Sensei.

TWENTY-ONE

Hamish stared into his empty sake cup, so preoccupied in thought that he did not realize Hiro had risen and come to stand by his side, holding the decanter – ready to provide a refill. When it became obvious that Hamish was unaware of his presence, Hiro returned to his place on the tatami. And after Toshiro observed this bit of silent theater, he decided to speak.

"Are you not well today, Gakusei?"

Still, there was no response from Hamish. Toshiro repeated the question – more loudly, after which Hamish looked up, as if he were coming out of a deep sleep.

"Oh......sorry, Sensei. I reckon my mind was somewhere else."

"And where might that *somewhere else* be, Gakusei?"

At first Hamish appeared perplexed by the question, but then he responded slowly, haltingly.

"Last night......I looked at the calendar and noticed ......my ship leaves for San Francisco in less than one month."

"And *that* causes you sadness, Gakusei? Do you not yearn for your home, friends, studio?"

"I....reckon so."

"Have you not accomplished your journey's purpose – to impart your skill to your employer's staff?"

Hamish looked blankly into Toshiro's eyes. Then,

he blinked several times, appearing to have returned to the conversation at hand.

"I reckon I came here for an *adventure* more than anything else, although I did right by my employer – I did teach his staff everything I know about photography. And they learned mighty quick, I must say! But any joy from that went away when I learned I had been gulled into being part of his secret, dirty business."

"You had no control over that, Gakusei. You were honorable in meeting your obligation to your employer. *He* will have to answer one day for his dishonorable action – if not to the authorities, then through the mysterious actions of *karma*."

"Karma?"

"Let us just say *delayed punishment*, delivered by Fate – and leave it at that. I am less concerned for bogus Prince Kashiwara, than I am for you. You say you came to Japan for an adventure. Did you not find one here?"

Hamish's face began to flush, but he had determined the previous evening to be as candid as possible with Toshiro during his last few weeks in his presence – no matter how embarrassing.

"My adventure, Sensei, really began the day I met *you*," he sputtered – nonetheless uncomfortable speaking so frankly to another man.

Toshiro paused to sip his sake and ponder Hamish's statement, before speaking again. "And what specific adventure did Hiro and I take you upon, Gakusei?"

Hamish again struggled to find the words. No one he knew in San Francisco talked of such matters. Life there was more practical: work, eat, sleep, drink – and visit the brothel when coins filled one's pocket. Here,

Toshiro wanted to talk of so much more. *Were these two nations even on the same planet?"*

"Um......well, *art* I reckon was the first thing. You raised some mighty vexatious questions about what it really is. You even challenged *my* art, picture-taking!"

Toshiro smiled. "Often in serious discussions, one challenges in order to provoke further thought. And since you have apparently revisited that issue over time, I would say my strategy bore fruit – did it not?"

Now it was Hamish's turn to smile. "I reckon."

"But we talked of so much more than art, Gakusei."

"Yes, Sensei. I learned many things about your customs, history, people, and this land – but *so* much more is left to know. I reckon that's why I'm a mite sad about having to leave so soon."

"What more would you have liked to learn, Gakusei?"

Hamish glanced in Hiro's direction, not having planned to do so deliberately, and then answered.

"Mostly about the samurai way of life."

"The samurai way of life? Gakusei, *that* is learned over the course of a lifetime – not during a visit of several months!"

Feeling chastised, Hamish sank deep down on the tatami, appearing much smaller than normal. This reaction on his part concerned Toshiro, as it was not his intention to humiliate Hamish, who was his guest.

"Let me explain more clearly, Gakusei, what is involved in absorbing the samurai way. I accept responsibility for not having done so in the past, when imparting bits of information to you about my noble profession."

Toshiro then motioned to Hiro to fetch the sake

decanter and refill any cups not already brimming with the brew. After Hiro had completed the task, Toshiro continued.

"Hiro, my Page, has been here for over five years. Shortly after the Tokugawa Shogunate fell and the New Government started legislating the samurai out of existence, he appeared at my gate. Day after day he returned, begging Mr. Ohsugi to admit him for an audience with me. I repeatedly refused, desirous to see no one at such a disastrous time for my proud profession. But the lad's persistence wore me down, and one day I told Mr. Ohsugi to admit him, for a brief audience. He has been with me ever since."

Hamish's eyes widened. "What about Hiro's family? Weren't they mighty concerned when he did not return home?"

"Ah, Gakusei – ever the practical American! Even if they had been alive, they would have understood the yearning of his soul for self-understanding and mastery of the world around him. But as it was, he had recently been orphaned and therefore was destitute and hungry – but not merely for food and shelter. I immediately recognized his voracity to live a better, fuller, more-meaningful life. Even though there was little hope he would be able to practice the skills I taught him – beyond these walls, he would be a better man as a result."

Hamish glanced at Hiro and was certain he could detect the gratitude and affection Hiro felt for his Master – having been chosen to live and learn in his presence.

"However," Toshiro continued, "even after all this time Hiro has but skimmed the surface in his education and training. So how can *you* allow yourself to be disappointed that you did not learn more in such a short time? The samurai way involves a lifetime of learning, struggle, victory and sometimes, *defeat.*"

Hamish was overcome by Toshiro's words, for reasons he did not fully understand. His chest began to heave and fall rapidly, and he had to struggle to maintain his composure. Toshiro recognized his distress and more-gently continued.

"Tell me, Gakusei, in the short time we have left together, what is it that you might learn from me that could stay with you the rest of your life?"

Hamish sat in silence for what appeared to be a very long time. Then, he responded. "I'm mighty impressed with your control, your discipline. You don't seem tossed about, hither and yon – like something bobbing on the ocean waves."

"I see. And would you like to perhaps make a small start in the area of self-discipline, while you are still with us?"

"Yes, Sensei, but I'm graveled as to how that can be done *now.*"

"*I* know, or rather *we* know – Hiro and I."

Hamish looked from one to the other, puzzled.

Toshiro continued. "Since early in your visits to my villa, it has been clear to us that you cannot control your lustful urges."

Hamish quickly sat upright on the tatami, uncertain as to what might follow. "*Lustful urges,* Sensei?"

"Yes – such as during your early visits, when you could not bear to look upon Hiro's magnificent countenance without being visibly aroused. We noticed, even though you were fully clothed. Later, we observed your similar response during our communal bath, when you were shown Kashiwara's erotic wares – and as recently as during the harvest/fertility festival. Your visible state of arousal on such occasions made it all too clear that you lack the discipline to control yourself in such situations. Your desires are normal and natural – mind you, but a samurai chooses when and where they will be acted upon. *He* is not randomly buffeted about by such impulses. But perhaps in the short time you will be remaining with us, we can begin to teach you how to instill a bit of self-discipline at such stimulating times. And to prove these impulses may be duly acted upon when *you* are in control – to my personal satisfaction, I shall reward you with a night such as you have never known."

"Never known, Sensei?"

"Yes, Gakusei. If you can impress me with your steadfastness in this matter, then once I am fully satisfied, you will spend an evening here with me, until the dawn breaks the next day. And you will experience the joy and satisfaction that comes when a man is ruled by himself – not by fate, circumstance, not the laws nor morals of others. Do you wish to begin your new lessons next time we meet – knowing the reward which awaits the successful mastery of your lustful urges?"

Hamish nodded slowly, still somewhat confounded by Toshiro's unexpected proposal.

TWENTY-TWO

"When you have lustful thoughts which cause you to become visibly aroused while in the presence of others, Gakusei, close your eyes and try to imagine a large white pearl lying upon a piece of black silk. Concentrate on that serene image and perhaps you will avoid the embarrassment you have experienced in my presence and Hiro's."

Hamish closed his eyes and attempted to follow Toshiro's instructions. However, he was extremely tense and anxious – for Toshiro had insisted he wear nothing but a short *happi coat* during this initial self-discipline exercise, which would obviously expose his genital area when he sat cross-legged on the tatami. It was clear to him that Toshiro desired to be able to easily and quickly view any uncontrollable excitement on his part.

After a period of closed-eyed concentration, Hamish reported, "Sensei, I see the pearl and feel mighty relaxed now."

"Do you, Gakusei? Then open your eyes and look about the room."

When Hamish did so, he discovered that both Toshiro and Hiro had quietly removed *their* happi coats and now stood before him wearing only fundoshi. Their revealing garments instantly reminded him of his arousal during the recent festival – and to make the scene appear even more erotic, his companions stood side-by-side with their arms tightly wrapped around each other's waist.

This image proved too sensual for Hamish and his aroused member began to swell between his exposed legs.

"Ah, Gakusei, you will need to concentrate more intently upon the pearl. But *that* is something you may practice tonight back at Kashiwara's guesthouse. For now, let us attempt another exercise, one which has been employed for centuries in the training of young monks in isolated monasteries. They too must be taught to face down their inappropriate carnal reactions to persons and objects, in public. This exercise consists of a series of repetitive chants, over a long period of time, while seated in the *lotus position*. Here, let me show you how simple it will be for you to assume this position, since you are already sitting cross-legged."

Toshiro approached, and with his near-naked body just inches from Hamish's face, placed the latter's hands upon his lap and showed him how to lightly rest the fingers of his right hand upon the upturned fingers of his left.

"This position represents *purity*, and will aid you in your chanting," Toshiro said, after he was satisfied all was in order. And then Toshiro taught him a common chanting sequence which was to be repeated aloud until he was told to stop. But after what appeared to Hamish an interminable duration, the boredom of the exercise encouraged his mind to wander. Therefore, when later exposed again to Toshiro and Hiro's erotic *tableaux vivant*, he once more became visibly aroused.

After several hours had passed with little success,

everyone was exhausted and Hamish was advised to return to Kashiwara's villa and practice these exercises there, before his next visit.

But during the following session, he again failed to control his urges through either chanting or several other methods he had been taught.

"I believe, Gakusei, if we are to have any hope of your exhibiting self-control in this matter before you leave this land forever, we must accelerate your training. Are you able to come here more often than twice weekly?"

"A strange thing, Sensei – Kashiwara no longer pays much mind to my comings and goings. He still wants me at the workshop on Wednesdays, Thursdays and Fridays, but doesn't question me anymore about the other days. When I'm there, I still work mighty hard with my assistants and the postcard printers – and I'm still taking portraits of folks there who Kashiwara doesn't consider important enough to be sent to my studio at his villa. There are a few who also come to the villa, but he told me he thinks the novelty of a photographic portrait is beginning to wear off among the rich folks in these parts, because so many have had one taken lately. So I believe I can come here as often as you like, from Saturdays through Tuesdays."

"Excellent, Gakusei, for the task of instilling you with a modicum of self-discipline before your departure will have little chance of success without greater effort and concentration on your part. In fact, we have decided – Hiro and I, more drastic measures are now in order where others have failed."

Hamish cast a quizzical look in Toshiro's direction, a bit unsettled by the phrase, *drastic measures*.

"Drastic measures, Sensei?"

"Yes, Gakusei – it is time, we believe, for the *ordeal by roses*."

"Ordeal.....what, Sensei?"

Toshiro nodded to Hiro, who went behind a nearby screen and brought forth dark pink blossoms attached to what appeared to be the stalks of a bush.

"These are our popular *rosa rugosa* – wild roses that are plentiful in Japan. They grow on bushes and like all roses, have prickly thorns."

Hamish stared at the objects, at first confused because they looked nothing like the long-stemmed beauties he frequently encountered in the flower stalls back home on Market Street. But then he realized they were akin to the wild roses which were plentiful in the California countryside.

Before he could speak, Toshiro continued.

"Centuries of training in self-discipline have taught us that sometimes a bit of *pain* might be necessary in order for *learning* to occur. Here, the pain will be delivered in the form of prickly thorns striking your tender back – until you show evidence of self-control in the matter at hand."

Hamish's lower jaw dropped, reflecting his amazement at Toshiro's suggestion. He immediately thought of San Francisco – a wild and wooly town if there ever were one. A town with frequent muggings, robberies, and shootouts in saloons which often left one or more persons dead. But none of that seemed to compare with some of the strange behavior he had seen in Japan *and* what Toshiro was now suggesting.

"I'm in a hugger-mugger, Sensei. I'm mighty graveled. Nothing like you're suggesting goes on in San Francisco, even though it can be a right-wild place at times. A person doesn't dare walk along the wharf alone late at night – for fear of waking up on a boat to

Lord knows where. And you don't flash your money in the open – any time of day or night. But *whipping* with thorny roses? No one back home would dream of such a thing!"

"Ah, but remember Gakusei, you are now in a very different world. However, the choice is yours. Here, drink some sake while you contemplate your level of sincerity in this matter. The desire to travel a well-disciplined path in life can only come from *within*, it cannot be imposed against your will."

Hamish was humbled by Toshiro's words, feeling he had failed this admirable person who had befriended him beyond anything a foreigner could expect – especially in a land long-closed to the outside world. He slowly drained his sake cup, and then replied.

"I'm a mite fearful – but yes, the *ordeal by roses*, Sensei."

Toshiro smiled. He then told Hamish to stand up and remove his happi coat – leaving him stark naked. Streams of sunlight penetrated the shoji screens which provided privacy from the outdoors, and they made the golden hairs on Hamish's chest, arms, thighs and genital area appear to glow. Unknown to him, at that moment, Toshiro and Hiro were both employing mental exercises to control their own lustful urges.

"You will stand still while Hiro holds the rose branches and waits to see if you are stimulated beyond your ability to control yourself, Gakusei. If you cannot, you will feel the sting of the thorns."

Hamish nodded slowly, nervously.

"And your temptation will be to watch the long-secret *sword dance of the samurai*."

Now Hamish began to tremble a bit, as he thought about the sharpness of Toshiro's treasured long and short samurai swords. But then he found himself wondering how such *cold* objects could evoke feelings of lust, temptation?

Soon, his unspoken question was answered, as Toshiro threw off his happi coat – revealing he wore but a fundoshi underneath. He then picked up his *short* sword and began to dance with it. After a time he pointed it toward his fundoshi and Hamish feared he was about to stab himself! But all he did was use it to put a tear in the garment. As the dance progressed, Toshiro employed the sword to shred the fundoshi repeatedly – until the remaining bits of cloth fell away from his body. For his part, Hamish was so shocked by this bizarre performance and terrified Toshiro would hurt himself, he did not exhibit the slightest sign of arousal. And he retained this state even when the now-naked Toshiro began to treat the sword as if it were a lover, holding it tenderly against his body as he danced with it and caressed it. When Toshiro was finished, he looked at Hamish, observed his flaccid state, and smiled.

"Ah, Gakusei, you have resisted the temptation I sent your way, and thus avoided the shedding of your blood."

Hamish glanced at Hiro, who was now lowering the thorny rose branches with which he had been poised to strike at any time. Hamish was certain he could detect disappointment in Hiro's eyes, for having been deprived of the chance to draw blood. Intuitively, Hamish recognized this was a *sadistic* exercise, but he lacked the sophistication to label it as such.

And then, Toshiro broke the brief silence.

"I believe *that* is enough for today, but I must be sure this was not an anomaly – and so you will be tested one last time. If you prevail in controlling your erotic urges again, then we shall plan for your *reward*."

While he awaited the final test, back at Kashiwara's villa, Hamish wondered about the mighty-weird business in which he was now enmeshed. Was it all a dream or were there many other people who lived in such a manner – engaged in open conversation about their sexual urges and ways to control them? He also continued to be unsettled over the manner in which his samurai friend obviously viewed his own rules as the only ones which mattered, eschewing those of the outside world which was destroying the samurai way of life. At least that appeared to Hamish to be Toshiro's continual message.

Soon, however, the time arrived for his return to Toshiro's villa, where he hoped he would successfully meet his final challenge. There, he was greeted by Toshiro in the nude, after Mr. Ohsugi escorted him from the gate to the house.

"Join me in freedom today, Gakusei. Embrace your natural instincts and throw off the strictures of pedestrian society!"

Hamish disrobed and Toshiro led him to a small room where an opaque folding screen was placed several feet away.

"Are you familiar with the *Legend of Saint Sebastian*, Gakusei?"

"Saint who?"

"Ah, yes – *your* ancestors were among those who rebelled against Rome, so you do not know of Sebastian. Still, a well-educated man strives to learn all he can of the world and its people – both friends and foes. But let me clarify the matter for you. Sebastian was a Centurian in ancient Rome, who converted to Christianity. He was rewarded for his service to the

Emperor Diocletian by promotion to the Pretorian Guard. When he later protested the cruel acts of Diocletian toward others, he was condemned to be shot through with arrows and afterwards was left for dead. For many Sebastian *cultists* in Europe – and increasingly here in Japan, his martyrdom ended *there*. And the image of his naked body, shot through with arrows has been replicated and lusted over by his followers for generations. In reality, he recovered from those wounds and lived to confront the Emperor once more – in keeping with the desire for martyrdom which saints tend to have in great abundance. This time Diocletian was so enraged by Sebastian's accusations – as well as the shock that he had survived his earlier ordeal, that he had him summarily bludgeoned to death on the spot and his body thrown into a nearby sewer. What I show you now is the image his followers celebrate instead."

With those words, Toshiro swiftly removed the folding screen, to reveal his naked Page, hands tied behind his back. Red liquid was pouring from what appeared to be wounds caused by arrowheads in his chest and abdomen. Hamish immediately started to feel his knees buckle beneath him, as Toshiro seized him under his arms, just in time.

"No, no, Gakusei – he is not injured. Look, it is but Mr. Ohsugi's cherry jam. And the protruding arrow feathers are but origami!"

Hamish regained his composure, stared at Hiro intently, and then turned to Toshiro, confused by it all.

"Go, go Gakusei – to Hiro. As your final test while I observe you, use your mouth and tongue to remove the *arrow feathers* and lick his wounds until you have removed all the blood-red fluid from his body. Only then will Hiro be *whole* again and safe. And if you conduct yourself with manly grace and self-restraint, your ordeal will also be over, at last. And the next time we meet, you will receive your reward."

Later, back at Kashiwara's villa, Hamish relived the moments which followed, as his teeth pulled away the origami and his tongue lapped up every drop of Ohsugi's bogus blood. And after the Page was *restored to life*, Toshiro and Hiro bowed deeply to Hamish – signaling he had passed the final test. Then for the first time in all the weeks they had shared sake, Toshiro raised the traditional Japanese toast in Hamish's presence – *Kampai!*

Hamish was well aware at the time that the staged scene of sensual torture did not arouse him. In fact, he considered it so silly that his greatest problem that day was stifling his laughter, so as not to offend the others. In addition, any hint of mixing pleasure with pain dulled his lust, for he did not associate them with each other. Such a combination of emotions and images had not been encountered by him back home at the bordello, and he therefore found nothing stimulating about the experience. In fact, he actually felt rather foolish and embarrassed by it all. But he would likely have submitted to almost *anything*, in order to earn the reward of a whole evening in Toshiro's samurai arms.

TWENTY-THREE

Hamish sat back in the jinrikisha and studied the note Hiro had prepared for him several months earlier, under Toshiro's direction. On one side the Japanese characters directed jinrikisha runners to Toshiro's villa – where he was now headed, and on the other to Kashiwara's. It was with a twinge of sadness that he realized he would likely only use it several more times before his ship sailed back to San Francisco in two weeks. *Perhaps I'll keep it as a souvenir of my adventure here*, he mused.

Toshiro had instructed him to eat an early dinner at Kashiwara's, so they could dispense with that task beforehand. And he also insisted Hamish had to come on *this* night – a *Friday*, even though he had been engaged all day at Kashiwara's workshop. He would rather have faced this highly-anticipated evening under less-exhausting circumstances, but dared not say or do anything to delay or interrupt tonight's events. For he was about to embark upon an act he would never have considered back home in San Francisco – having sexual relations with a *man*!

But every encounter with Toshiro had been a fascinating one – opening new doors, showing him new pathways, and the *reward* he was about to receive would be the crowning glory for the modest self-discipline he had just recently exhibited, to the samurai master's satisfaction.

He came out of his reverie when he realized the runner had stopped before the familiar gate – the gate through which he had entered a truly exotic world in the not-too-distant past.

And soon, much to his surprise, Toshiro himself admitted him at the gate, after he rang the now-familiar bell. After reciprocal bows, Hamish followed Toshiro into the house, as his eyes darted to and fro, looking for signs of the presence of Hiro and Mr. Ohsugi. The ever-observant samurai answered his unspoken question.

"No one else is about tonight. This night is only about *us*."

Hamish smiled in relief, for as his anticipation had mounted throughout the day, he had hoped the evening would belong only to the two of them.

"We shall start with the cleansing ritual, enjoying my country's unique method for preparing one's body before entering the bath. And of course, you are by now familiar with the procedure."

Hamish nodded and followed Toshiro to the small room where the tiled floor was fitted with a drain, and furnished with low wooden stools and water buckets. They quickly disrobed and hung their clothing on nearby wall pegs.

"Here, Gakusei, allow me to pour this bucket of water over you so I may work up a lather all over your body."

Toshiro motioned for Hamish to sit on one of the small stools and first washed his hair and face, quickly rinsing off the lather with clear water. Then, with his eyes wide open, Hamish submitted himself to Toshiro's strong hands – lathering and massaging his chest, arms, torso, abdomen, legs, hands and feet. And then he motioned for Hamish to stand while he did the same within the crevices of his buttocks and in the area of his groin.

Hamish began to respond to this intimate contact, but before he could evince embarrassment, Toshiro reminded him of the purpose of this meeting.

"Have no embarrassment tonight, Gakusei. You have earned the right to enjoy your lustful urges at will and display them openly. For tonight we are assured they are within your control now, and it is you who deliberately acts upon *them*, rather than allowing them to direct *you*. Along with me, you have chosen the time and the place, and together we shall share no embarrassment – only joy!"

With that said, Toshiro poured clear water all over Hamish's body until the soapsuds disappeared down the drain.

"Now, Gakusei, show your Sensei what you have just learned."

Hamish eagerly attempted to duplicate the motions of Toshiro, and when he reached the latter's groin, Toshiro's swollen member indicted he also felt the full sensuality of this intimate encounter.

When Toshiro's body was fully rinsed of the soap residue, they entered the nearby tub, already filled with pristine clear water. It was only then that Hamish noticed the small tray upon which was placed a sake decanter and cups – within easy reach. Toshiro poured and as they slowly drained the decanter they stared into each other's eyes, as their respective members visibly swelled – with their foreskins retracting in the process.

After they emerged from the tub and dried off, Toshiro pointed to a pair of garments hanging on another of the chamber's wall pegs, and they each put one on. Hamish was puzzled for a moment, as the garment was too long to be a happi coat, yet too short to be a kimono, since it ended just below his knee. The ever-vigilant Toshiro immediately clarified the matter.

"These garments are *yukata* – somewhat akin to a lightweight cotton kimono, but shorter. They are often worn after bathing. Now come, Gakusei, to my sleeping chamber," Toshiro beckoned, as he held out his hand to Hamish, who eagerly took it.

Toshiro's sleeping quarters consisted of a small, sparsely-furnished room – with a pallet in the middle of the floor, a simple flower arrangement on a low stand, and a small scroll hanging on one wall. Multiple burning candles were placed around the room, causing the bright red silk cover on the pallet to appear to be on fire. Hamish was also struck by the heavy scent in the room. He asked Toshiro if it came from the candles.

"No, Gakusei. Do you not see the incense burner over in the far corner of the room? It is filled with exotic sandalwood incense, a *calming* scent which was a gift to Japan from ancient China centuries ago. It is another of the customs the Buddhist monks brought to us."

Hamish nodded and inhaled the aromatic fumes, which when mixed with the sake he had consumed, served to drive all inhibitions from him. Then he stepped closer to examine the lone piece of art in the room – the wall scroll.

It was a narrow, vertical scroll, which appeared to depict a large cat stalking among tall bamboo. He studied the animal's body, and piercing blue eyes, and was puzzled. He turned to Toshiro.

"Sensei, what is this creature?"

Toshiro smiled. "It is a *tiger*, as imagined by a Japanese artist who had never seen one in the flesh. Tigers are not native to Japan. About fifteen years ago a Dutch merchant brought several to the zoo in Edo's Ryokoku District and they caused a sensation – artists rushed to paint them. But for decades they had been known here only by legend and this one was painted many years ago from imagination by an artist named *Kikugawa Eizan*. Thus, the body is not completely accurate and the eyes are *blue* instead of tannish-yellow."

Hamish stared at the scroll more closely, while absorbing this information. "I can see why I was graveled at first – the blue eyes and the unusual body – so different from what I have seen at the zoo back in San Francisco."

"Actually, Gakusei, the animal's blue eyes were what led me to purchase it several years ago. The more I stared at them, the more I was overcome by the feeling that one day I would be visited by someone with *blue* eyes – *aoi me-san*, in our language. On some level, it appeared to be a talisman whose ownership would hasten that day."

"And did your *blue eyes* come, Sensei?"

Toshiro now laughed more-heartily than he ever had in Hamish's presence.

"Of course, Gakusei – he was *you*! And so tonight you will be called *aoi me ga toru* – the blue-eyed one, and just as the tiger in the scroll stalks among the bamboo, so shall you slither and meander among *my* bamboo."

And before Hamish could anticipate what was about to happen, Toshiro grasped his hand and placed it upon his fully erect member. Hamish's blue eyes widened as he allowed Toshiro to direct his grasped hand up and down the samurai's phallic rod several times, to the pleasure of both of them. Then Toshiro removed Hamish's hand and led him to the pallet. He pulled him down onto it and began to stroke, caress, embrace and kiss Hamish – in a most forceful manner.

Hamish had no idea how long this foreplay lasted, for he chose to simply surrender himself to Toshiro and follow his lead. At some point, Toshiro whispered into the ear he had been vigorously licking.

"Tonight, *aoi me ga toru*, I shall introduce you to the joys of *tantric* sex, as described in the *Kama Sutra*."

Hamish pulled himself away and stared at Toshiro's face. "What is *that*?"

And so the sensual samurai began to explain in a soft-spoken, calm, reassuring and simple manner, a brief history of the tantric view that sex is the totally of *All*.

"The teachings of the Kama Sutra were brought to Japan by Buddhists during the Heian Period in the twelfth century – having originated in India. For several centuries thereafter, these teachings were outlawed here, but like all other forbidden great knowledge – they simply went underground until more-receptive times. Is this not the cycle of the world's greatest revelations? Anyway, *Kama Sutra* literally means *aphorisms of love, pleasure and sensual gratification* – and tonight I shall introduce you to several of them. You have already experienced some basic practices during your visits here – group bathing, massage, and tonight deep kissing, licking, and caressing the member of one's lover."

Hamish could feel his pale face starting to flush, and he struggled to prevent the crimson from spreading from ear-to-ear – as it often did on such emotional occasions. But Toshiro appeared to pay no mind to it, instead continuing with his *instruction*.

"Here, come and entwine our limbs together, while I gaze into your blue eyes and we kiss passionately. This is called *Jataveshtitaka* – the twining of the creeper."

As with the other positions yet to be demonstrated, Hamish lost all sense of time – taken up by the moment, completely absorbed by the joyful novelty of this night. At some point, however, Toshiro disengaged and continued his lesson.

"Now let me place one foot upon one of yours and my other foot on your thigh. Then let me pass one of my arms around your back and place the other upon your shoulders. And in this position, we may kiss and caress each other. This is called *Vrikshadhirudhaka* – the climbing of the tree."

After a time determined solely by Toshiro, he pulled apart from Hamish and spoke again.

"Now, we will lie stretched out upon the pallet with our arms and legs wrapped tightly around each other. This is called *Tila-Tandulaka* – the mixture of sesame and salt."

Throughout the time spent in these positions, Hamish eagerly responded to Toshiro's kisses, caresses, exploring tongue and fingers – by mimicking them as best he could in his role as novice. But he was not prepared for what came next.

Toshiro pressed Hamish down upon the pallet, facing upward. He spread the blue-eyed one's legs, raised them and with a well-practiced thrust of his engorged member entered the orifice Hamish had never associated with lovemaking. He was about to cry out in pain, but the samurai's hot mouth tightly covered his own. At the same time, Toshiro positioned their arms and legs so they were now locked in a total embrace. Soon, the last words Hamish would hear before he lost consciousness were, "This is *Kshiraniraka* – the flower duet."

TWENTY-FOUR

When Hamish awoke the next morning, he found himself wrapped tightly in Toshiro's arms. He desperately wanted to leave the pallet to relieve himself but was fearful he would disturb the sleeping samurai. However, his discomfort soon caused his body to twitch involuntarily – just enough to stir Toshiro from his slumber.

"Ah, aoi me ga toru, it is so pleasant to awaken and find you in my arms," he whispered as he kissed Hamish's face several times.

"Sensei, I'm mighty pleased myself, but I must go to the chamber pot right quick!"

Toshiro smiled, "Then go – and I shall eagerly await your return."

Hamish retrieved the yukata he wore the night before and put it on, not knowing if Mr. Ohsugi or Hiro were about. He then rushed to the small closet where he quickly voided into the pot, before returning to Toshiro's pallet.

"Aoi me ga toru, tell me – was last evening a pleasant one for you?"

Hamish's brow began to furrow, as he tried to find words to explain the unexpected combination of pleasure and pain he had experienced the night before.

"It was mighty nice, Sensei – but that last part.....I

did not expect anything like *that*, and begging your pardon but it did hurt."

A grave expression crossed Toshiro's face, as he took Hamish's head in both his hands. "That was your first time with a man, was it not?"

Hamish nodded.

"It will become easier, should you desire to pursue such delights back in San Francisco. But you must learn to *relax* throughout the act."

"Truth be told, that last part did not pleasure me, Sensei. All the rest did – but not that. I reckon, though, that you enjoyed it."

"Yes, I do enjoy deflowering a novice – although in the past they have all been much younger than you, and more pliant. However, did you truly enjoy the rest of the evening? The ancient custom of male love has been long-endorsed by the samurai and is now being driven underground by the new Government – as it rushes to adopt the morals of the puritanical West."

"Oh yes, it was mighty pleasurable, Sensei."

"Then when you return home you must decide which of the delights I taught you last night you wish to continue enjoying, however surreptitiously. The matter is strictly in your hands now."

Hamish nodded, uncertain he would ever have the opportunity for such male coupling in rough-and-tumble San Francisco – a town whose rich and powerful leaders and church folk embodied the Western morals Toshiro despised.

"But for now, let us break the evening's fast. Let me put on my yukata also and we shall go to the other room where Mr. Ohsugi will serve us."

As they walked to the area of the house where meals were served, Toshiro called out to Mr. Ohsugi, in Japanese. The old former samurai – now but a household servant, quickly appeared and absorbed his master's verbal orders before disappearing for a time. Toshiro and Hamish then turned their attention to the beautiful courtyard scene, now in clear view because Mr. Ohsugi had slid open several of the shoji panels which provided nighttime privacy.

When the latter returned, he brought eggs, fish paste, toast and tea. Hamish and Toshiro both ate heartily – their gustatory ardor second only to that of their sexual zeal the evening before. Later, after Mr. Ohsugi cleared everything away except for a fresh pot of tea and two clean cups, Toshiro spoke.

"Sadly, you will be gone from here in two weeks time, Gakusei. I hope you have learned much of value under my tutelage. I surmised a strong desire in you for adventure and enlightenment during our early visits and thereafter attempted to share all I could with you during your brief stay in our land."

Hamish quickly responded, "Oh yes, Sensei, Yes! You took me on a great adventure – beyond anything I expected or could imagine. I'm forever beholden to you."

Toshiro nodded and then replied, "I am pleased to hear that, aoi me ga toru. And since my people practice the principle of *reciprocity* in social situations, there is a great favor you can provide me in return – one which would please me immensely. And if you elect to do it, you will owe me nothing more, for our souls will have exchanged courtesies of equal value."

Hamish stared at Toshiro, puzzled. Then he asked, "What can I possibly give you in return for your kindness and friendship?"

"Something rather simple, for one with your modern skills – it is now Saturday, and on Monday morning I would like you to come here and photograph me."

Hamish brightened – at last the portrait of Toshiro which Kashiwara had long desired! "Do you mean a portrait like Hiro's, Sensei?"

"Oh, no. This is something very special and unusual. I would like you to photograph an ancient ceremony. I should say *part* of one – since your cumbersome developing process will not make it possible for you to photograph *all* the stages in the ceremony in rapid succession. And so, you will only photograph the beginning and the ending."

"Just two exposures, Sensei?"

"Yes. I have thought upon this matter for awhile and believe the best way to achieve my goal is for you to come here early Monday morning, with your darkroom cart. You may park it in the alley behind my villa. Mr. Ohsugi will assist you with your equipment, and Hiro will tell you when to expose the first glass plate – as I am not allowed to speak during the ceremony. After you have done so, you will return to your darkroom cart and begin the tedious process of developing the plate before the coating dries. When I am ready for you to photograph the conclusion of the ritual, Mr. Ohsugi will fetch you and you will make the second exposure, upon Hiro's command. Is this acceptable to you?"

"Of course, Sensei – after all you have done for me it is a mighty small favor on my part."

"Good. Now there are several more instructions. I wish you to print only *two* images from each plate and the next morning, Tuesday, deliver them and the plates here. And no one else is to see them or know of this event. Is that amenable to you, also?"

"Certainly, Sensei. I've been graveled over how

• The Meiji Prince •

to repay you for your hospitality these past months. I had even thought of offering to take your portrait and give it to you as a gift – even though I don't reckon picture-taking meets your standard for *art*."

They both laughed at this, recalling Hamish's early visit when Toshiro challenged him on this very point. And then, Toshiro suddenly turned serious and spoke in a near-whisper.

"There are times, Gakusei, when *any* tool must be used in battle."

Hamish was once again at a loss for words, uncertain as to the meaning of yet another cryptic phrase from Toshiro's lips. But he had no chance to ask for clarification, as Toshiro rose from the tatami and bowed deeply, indicating it was time for Hamish to leave. After the latter had changed back into his Western clothing, Toshiro walked him to the gate, looked deeply into his blue eyes, and kissed him full on the mouth with much passion.

His last words to Hamish that morning, as he opened the gate, were "Remember, I wish you to speak to no one of Monday's business – before *or* afterward."

As Hamish rode in the jinrikisha back to Kashiwara's villa, he was elated to know he finally had a suitable way to repay his gracious *host* – for he considered Toshiro to have filled that role while he was in Japan, not the duplicitous *Prince*. And then he remembered that the Japanese placed great store upon the wrapping of gifts. During his stay he had seen several examples of professionally-wrapped gifts which he considered almost worthy of the label – *works of art*. And momentarily he was prepared to hire such a person to wrap the photographs and plates before he delivered them to Toshiro. But then he remembered the samurai's injunction that no one see them, and he had to discard that option. Happily, he next recalled that during one of his forays to the Ginza, he had seen large square pieces of cloth which were sold for wrapping gifts. He once watched a store clerk place a newly-purchased item in the center of one, pull up all four corners, and then tie a knot at the top.

"Ginza, Ginza", he shouted at the jinrikisha runner, who smiled, bowed and turned his vehicle in that direction and away from Kashiwara's villa.

Later, when Hamish was in a shop which sold such items, the minimally English-speaking clerk told him they were called *furoshiki*. And he further related that after removing the gift, the cloth could be used for many other purposes by the recipient.

Hamish's selection then became one largely of price and color, for there were a variety of choices among the shop's stock. The sales clerk began to interpret the Japanese meaning of the various colors, in case that were relevant to the gift-giving occasion, but Hamish politely interrupted him – pointing to a *blue* one. The clerk smiled and said, "Blue is the color of *peace* for us."

Hamish nodded quickly, indicating he wanted to purchase it. And on his way to Kashiwara's later, he thought about the multiple meanings of his color choice, for Toshiro. Surely, it would serve to remind his friend of the American *blue-eyed one* – his special Gakusei, long after he returned to California. And if there were but a single wish Hamish could bestow upon Toshiro – so obviously troubled by the suppression of his profession and the many changes in the world about him, it would be for a lifetime of peace.

TWENTY-FIVE

When Hamish entered the alley behind Toshiro's villa early Monday morning, he found Mr. Ohsugi waiting there – ready to tend to the horse pulling his darkroom cart.

After Hamish unloaded his camera and tripod, and connected the former to the latter, Mr. Ohsugi carried them into the house. Meanwhile, Hamish coated and sensitized the first glass plate, in the darkness of his little canvas-covered cart. He then carefully carried it into the house, where Mr. Ohsugi beckoned him to a folding screen in front of which he had placed the tripod-mounted camera. The old samurai then removed the folding screen, Hamish stepped forward, looked into the back hole and found himself gazing upon a very strange scene.

Toshiro was kneeling on the tatami, dressed in a white silk kimono. He also wore a white headband which had a red circle painted in the middle and black Japanese calligraphy on either side of it. Hamish recalled the red circle represented the *Rising Sun of Japan* – a symbol he had encountered all over Tokyo since his arrival.

Toshiro appeared to be staring at a small white bundle which lay on a low table before him – the latter also covered with a white cloth. The only other objects in the room were a plain shoji screen behind him, and a single yellow chrysanthemum in a clear glass vase on another low table – about six feet to Toshiro's right. As for Toshiro, he offered no acknowledgement of Hamish's presence – appearing to be in a trance, as he stared intently at the white bundle before him.

Suddenly, Hiro appeared, also dressed in a kimono of white silk, and promptly said to Hamish, "*Hai!*" – gesturing with his hand that the first plate now be exposed. Hamish opened the aperture and exposed the plate to the scene, while he covered the camera with a large black cloth to keep out extraneous light. He then took out his pocket watch and studied it closely, in order to monitor exposure time. When he decided the plate had been exposed long enough, he removed it and rushed back to the darkroom cart, in order to begin the developing process while he waited to be notified it was time to photograph the final stage of the ritual.

After a time, just as he was satisfied that the developing process was safely underway, Mr. Ohsugi appeared and signaled him to return to the ceremony. Hamish assumed the final stage of the mysterious ancient ritual was about to be played out, but when he returned he was surprised to find that Mr. Ohsugi had re-installed the folding screen – blocking his view of Toshiro. But soon he heard Hiro call out again, "*Hai!*" – at which time the old samurai swiftly removed the screen.

Hamish absorbed the horror of the scene before him almost immediately, and started to fall backward in a faint – but Mr. Ohsugi rushed forward to steady him and prevent him from tumbling to the floor. Of all the details Hamish would later remember of this terrible day, one small one would be his realization that the wizened old samurai was much stronger than he appeared. But then a sharp, second cry of "*Hai!*" from Hiro forced him to refocus his attention on the task at hand.

What Hamish saw before him now, as he tried to steady his hand, expose the plate and monitor the time on his pocket watch – would stay with him for years to come: Toshiro's headless body lay shoulder-down on the small table before him. Blood had poured all over its white cover, and his kimono also appeared to be saturated with it – indicating abdominal wounds. A few feet away, a round object *connected* to Toshiro's lifeless body by a trail of blood drops on the tatami, was covered by a white cloth. But being spared a view of Toshiro's severed head was small consolation for Hamish, who by then had turned his attention to Hiro. The Page stood beside his Master's body, holding the latter's long samurai sword – pointed downward, with blood visible on the blade. Tears were flowing down his beautiful face.

As soon as Hamish determined it was time to remove the glass plate and take it back to the darkroom cart, Mr. Ohsugi reinstalled the folding screen – thus removing the ghastly scene from Hamish's backward glance as he left the room. But that last image was *not* removed from his mind's eye, nor would it ever be.

In a state of shock, Hamish began to develop the plate. Sometime later, when he felt it was safe to transport both plates back to Kashiwara's villa, he directed the horse there. He spent most of the rest of the afternoon assuring that the development of these two precious – yet horrible, items was flawless. But by evening he was too exhausted and distressed to attempt to make the prints which had been requested.

He forced down a bit of the dinner Mrs. Saigo

brought him, and then fell upon his pallet. But sleep would not come easily that night. In addition to being plagued by recollections of the last scene he photographed, there were the unanswered questions: *Why did he do it? How could Toshiro give up his life – so ideal in many ways, despite the loss of his profession?* These and other unanswerable notions would haunt him throughout the restless night ahead.

In the morning, after a meager attempt at eating breakfast, he attended to printing the photographs requested by Toshiro at their last meeting. By the time that was done and they were hung up and drying, he was so exhausted he returned to his pallet – sleeping through lunch. As he lay down, he planned to deliver the promised package to Toshiro's villa in the late afternoon, after he awoke from his nap. Upon finding him so indisposed, Mrs. Saigo returned to her residence with the lunch tray she brought to the guesthouse – rather than disturb him. She determined she would prepare a larger-than-usual dinner for him that evening.

But his slumber was abruptly interrupted by Mr. Saigo in mid-afternoon. After bowing and apologizing to Hamish for disturbing his sleep, he indicated he had been sent by Prince Kashiwara to fetch him and take him to the workshop, where he was needed immediately. Hamish was annoyed to be roused on a day when he was normally not expected to be at the workshop, but Kashiwara *was* his employer and he knew his obligation under the circumstances.

As they rode to the workshop in Kashiwara's personal carriage, with Mr. Saigo holding the reins, Hamish wondered: *What can possibly be the emergency?* And he also worried that it might delay his planned delivery of the photographs and plates to Toshiro's villa until the *following* day.

As they pulled up to the workshop, Hamish noticed the *Closed* sign – written in English and Japanese, on the front door. However, Mr. Saigo urged him to enter anyway, and when he did, a loud cheer went up.

The Card Shop was filled with Kashiwara's employees – bowing to Hamish and shouting words of good cheer in Japanese, as well as a few in English. The latter came from Kashiwara and the Card Shop clerks, who were more conversant in English than most of the production line staff. And then Kashiwara stepped forward.

"Mr. Boyd – welcome to your surprise departure party! We had planned to hold it *next* week, but it occurred to me that you would likely be busy packing for your trip then – and perhaps also eager to visit some of the places nearby which you have been too busy to enjoy, during your labors. And so today, the Staff and I wish to thank you for the contribution you have made to the Firm's prosperity, by teaching us your skill and thereby enhancing our product inventory."

Immediately thereafter, sake cups were filled and passed around, after which Kashiwara raised a toast: *"Kampai! Sayonara! Kampai!"* – joined in by the others. As he drank, Hamish ruefully wondered which part of the product inventory was the focus of Kashiwara's gratitude. Surely, he referred to the *forbidden* wares, produced in secret and sold outside the law!

He then re-focused his attention on the event transpiring before him, signaling he also wished to raise a toast. After the sake cups were refilled, he bowed slowly to all present, being sure to turn around so as to include everyone – thanking his employer and co-workers for this wonderful send-off: "*Domo arigato! Domo arigato! Domo arigato!*" In the course of doing so, it occurred to him that two of his three photographic assistants were not there, but he assumed they were likely busy in the photographic studio, working on a project which could not be left unattended or delayed.

And then, Kashiwara brought forth an elaborately-wrapped gift, which Hamish was encouraged to open on the spot – contrary to Japanese custom. He did so reluctantly, as it seemed a shame to disturb the infinite care which had obviously been taken to present it so beautifully. However, since his well-wishers desired he do so, he first removed the thin gauze-like cloth which was held together by several elaborately-designed ribbons. Underneath, the package was wrapped again, in red silk. As he started to remove it, Kashiwara pointed out, "Red is the color of *celebration* in Japan." This led to Hamish bowing and uttering, "*Domo arigato*", again.

Eventually, he uncovered a carved wooden box, which contained an assortment of the postcards which had been produced from his own photographs, taken in and around Tokyo. He could not prevent himself from quickly calculating if it would fit inside one of his small trunks on the voyage home, and determined it would.

Kashiwara then led him to his Office, where a large assortment of food was spread out upon his desk, and several Western-style tables which had obviously been brought in for the occasion. Hamish was encouraged to fill his plate, alongside the Prince – and then the others followed their lead. At the same time, staff circulated continually with trays holding sake decanters, and more of the rice wine was pressed upon the guest of honor. Every time Hamish thought the party was coming to an end, more food arrived, more toasts were offered – usually in Japanese and therefore requiring translation sometimes. And the ever-present sake trays were always but a few inches away.

The usual hour for leaving work at day's end came and went, and with the passage of time the party became more raucous. Hamish could not help noticing, even in his sake–induced stupor, that he was seeing his usually staid, hard-working colleagues in a new light. And then, the lights went out for *him*, as everything turned black, and for Hamish the party was now over.

TWENTY-SIX

Upon waking the next morning, the first thing Hamish realized was that his head ached terribly. He pressed his hands against both sides of his skull, as he had been taught in childhood, but little relief followed.

And he also soon became aware of the fact that instead of waking up on his floor pallet at Kashiwara's guesthouse, he was in the latter's Office, stretched out upon a Western-style sofa his employer recently purchased for the comfort of foreign customers he wanted to impress. As soon as he could muster his strength, he stood up on wobbly legs and went to the door.

The most-talkative of the Shop's clerks was busy uncovering the merchandise displays, which had been shielded overnight by thin dustcovers. Upon seeing Hamish in the doorway, he immediately bowed. Hamish attempted to do so in return, but it was only a token bow – as his body ached too much for bending at that moment.

"What happened last night?" he asked the clerk.

The clerk laughed and replied, "Oh, Mr. Boyd – you had a wonderful departure party, but the *sake god* overwhelmed you and many of the others who will also have swollen heads today!"

Just then, several production-line workers arrived, also looking the worse for wear. They bowed to

Hamish, smiled weakly, and went straight to their work stations. Then the clerk spoke again.

"Prince Kashiwara bade me keep *this* safe for you, until you could retrieve it this morning." He then reached under the display counter and pulled out the postcard-filled wooden box Hamish had been given as a farewell gift.

"Thank you," Hamish uttered, adding "I must go to the toilet *now!*"

"Of course," the clerk responded, but he had one more item to relate. "After Mr. Saigo delivers the Prince here this morning, he has been instructed to take you back to your quarters, where you may more-comfortably overcome the mischief of the *sake god*."

"That's mighty thoughtful of him," Hamish answered, as he dashed off to the toilet.

When he returned, he found that the affable clerk had a cup of tea and a rice cake waiting for him. Hamish hungrily partook of this unexpected breakfast, and had just finished as Kashiwara arrived. After a brief good-natured review of the raucous party the night before, the Prince sent Hamish on his way, under Mr. Saigo's care.

As soon as he was back at his quarters, he cleaned himself up, wrapped the promised plates and photographs in the blue *furoshiki*, and hailed a jinrikisha in the street to take him to Toshiro's villa.

Several pulls on the bell beside the courtyard door finally led to its being opened. Much to Hamish's surprise, it was not Mr. Ohsugi who responded, but Hiro – dressed in a simple black kimono. The samurai Page stared so intently and silently at Hamish that the visitor began to feel Hiro was actually *glaring* at him.

Contrite over his delay in delivering the items Toshiro requested, Hamish spoke first.

"*Gomen-nasai,* I'm sorry," he uttered, as he simultaneously handed Hiro the package.

Hiro took it and half-turned away, apparently calling to Mr. Ohsugi in Japanese to come fetch it – for the servant quickly came and did so. And then Hiro spoke to Hamish.

"You were expected *yesterday.*"

"I was…..sick," Hamish sheepishly answered – deciding it was but a *half-lie,* in view of his drunken incapacitation.

Hiro looked skeptical and replied, "Mr. Ohsugi and I have to vacate this place by nightfall – I feared you would not return in time."

"By nightfall? Why?"

"The *Locusts of Kyoto* arrive tomorrow," Hiro responded, ruefully.

Hamish instinctively looked about, searching for signs of an approaching insect invasion in the air. Hiro perceived his misapprehension immediately and clarified.

"I speak of my Master's wife and children. Under Japanese law they have inherited this place and almost all of his estate."

Now, Hamish felt very sorry for both Hiro and Mr. Ohsugi – one an orphan and the other an old man who lost his professional status under the new Government.

"But where will you go? What will you do?"

"Yesterday, when it did not appear you were going to arrive, we visited my Master's solicitor. We took a sealed document he had advised us to share with the gentleman in the event of his death. The solicitor examined it and informed us we had each been left a modest stipend, within the limits of the law. Mr. Ohsugi has already made arrangements to live with his grandson, who is *also* employed by your *Prince*. He will contribute to the household expenses, using his stipend, but it will not last long. However, to his great joy and good fortune, Kashiwara has offered him a pushcart from which to hawk his souvenir postcards to foreigners and Japanese tourists, in Ueno Park."

Hamish absorbed this news and it momentarily caused him to reassess his ambivalent attitude toward Kashiwara.

"And yourself, Hiro? What will *you* do now?"

The Page appeared to sigh, slightly, and then he replied.

"I shall take lodging at a modest inn for the time being, while I consider my future. Of course, I cannot become apprenticed again to a samurai warrior, under *this* Government. And so, my Master's solicitor suggested that in view of my command of the English language, I might seek employment either as a teacher of English to the Japanese, or Japanese to American and British commercial travelers and tourists. He also suggested that I might serve as a tour guide, in view of the growing number of foreign visitors to our island nation."

It was only then that Hamish became consciously aware that: *Hiro speaks mighty fine English!*

"I didn't know you spoke English so well, Hiro. You only said a mite few words around me over these past months."

"My Master insisted I take lessons in the English language at the same time he did. He also told me many times that one can learn more from *listening* than from *talking*. In addition, he was fond of advising me not to allow others to know *everything* about myself – to keep part of me a mystery. It was a samurai tactic, he said."

"I'm sorry I did not have the chance to know you better, Hiro. I would like to be parting today as *friends*. It's mighty odd for me to say it, I reckon, but I believe I was even beginning to take up some of your samurai ways."

Upon hearing these words, Hiro sneered and laughed in a mocking manner.

"You, a samurai! Never in one thousand years! A samurai must always focus on his *giri* – his duty, and not put it after his *ninjo* – human feelings and emotions. It is not likely you will ever achieve such a state of mind and self-discipline!"

Hamish looked away from Hiro for a few moments, feeling unjustly and cruelly chastised and rebuked. Then he spoke again.

"I reckon you say that because I almost fainted Monday – but I've never seen such a sight as *that*. We don't do such things to people we love back home, and I believe you *loved* Toshiro."

Hiro was losing patience with this ignorant *barbarian*, but he continued.

"It was precisely out of *love* that I did as my Master commanded. And so once again, you have shown that you will never be able to understand the notion of duty before emotion."

Though stung by the charge, Hamish quietly responded, "In my own way, I loved Toshiro too."

"You refer to the night you shared his pallet? That honor should have been *mine* – for it was the *last* time my Master enjoyed such pleasure."

Hamish was now very perplexed.

"But he did not.....die until Monday! Didn't you lie with him on Saturday and Sunday?"

Hiro sighed again, and with obvious condescension uttered, "My Master immediately began the required *purification ritual* after you left. He was not allowed to engage further in such pleasures, under the tradition of samurai seppuku. And so it was *you, aoi me ga toru* – the blue-eyed one, who had the great honor of sharing his pallet for the last time, and not *I*."

Hamish did not know how to respond to this combination of rebuke, anguish, regret and loss on Hiro's part. And then a minor point crossed his mind, in a desperate attempt to continue this final conversation, however distressing.

"Can I ask why there was that single yellow chrysanthemum in the room when he died?"

Hiro struggled to be civil, tired of this conversation, but trying to remember the native etiquette he had been taught in childhood.

"The chrysanthemum is the official flower of Japan, and the Emperor sits upon the Chrysanthemum Throne. Also, yellow is the color of *courage*. And so, my Master honored both his country and Emperor at the same time that he exhibited his personal courage and bravery that morning."

And then, weary of talking to Hamish any further, Hiro tried to signal the end of the conversation by expressing again his anger over the delay in the delivery of the package to the villa – Toshiro's last request of the American.

"While I have been kneeling in mourning for my Master most of the past several days, you could not stay sufficiently vigilant to complete his last request of you, in a timely manner. Still, I am obligated to reward you, as my Master saw fit."

Hiro then half-turned and called for Mr. Ohsugi once more, who quickly returned to the courtyard, carrying a long, narrow, elegantly-wrapped object. He handed it to Hiro, who then bowed as he in turn handed it to Hamish. Hamish bowed and thanked him, using his limited Japanese vocabulary. At the same time, he was unable to prevent himself from mentally computing if it would fit inside one of his two small trunks, along with the gift from Kashiwara and his staff. And as soon as he did so, he imagined Toshiro mocking him: *Ever the practical American! Ever the practical American!*

Sensing that Hiro was desirous of ending their meeting, Hamish desperately tried to continue the conversation – hoping it would become friendly and less adversarial. But just as his mouth began to form words, Hiro took control of the awkward situation.

"I must retire now in order to carry out my Master's wishes regarding your professional efforts on his behalf."

Before Hamish could tell Hiro he did not understand what he was referring to, Hiro continued in rapid succession – as if he dared not delay what he was about to reveal.

"I must now atone for my loss of control during my Master's brave act of seppuku."

"*Your* loss of control?" Hamish said, with incredulity.

Hiro looked away, as if in shame, and then with much sadness in his voice, and tears forming in his eyes, came close and whispered in Hamish's ear.

"I delayed the sword, forcing my beloved Master to cry out *twice* for its merciful release – as his organs poured from his body!"

He then bowed slowly to Hamish, softly said, *Sayonara*, and closed the courtyard door in the face of his stunned American visitor.

TWENTY-SEVEN

Hamish's last week in Japan was left to his discretion – thanks to the generosity of Kashiwara. Packing took little time, for he was returning to America with only the two small trunks he originally brought with him. And since he had made no major purchases, they would accommodate the wooden box from Kashiwara and his staff that was filled with postcards of scenes of Tokyo he had taken, and also the gift from Toshiro which Hiro had given to him at their final meeting. The latter remained unopened, as Hamish could not yet bear to see what his dead samurai friend had left him.

During his last few days as a foreign visitor, Hamish revisited Ueno Park and other places of beauty and interest in and around Tokyo. He also dropped by the workshop several times, offering last-minute assistance. He found the Studio staff very busy and his former apprentices quite in control of matters.

They explained to him that the *Prince* had once again exhibited his business acumen when the demand for individual portraits started to wane recently. Kashiwara surmised that the initial novelty of the new technology had diminished – at the same time that those who had the ready-cash to rush in for a portrait had already done so. It would take awhile, he advised, for less-fortunate persons to save their *yen* and eventually come in for a studio photograph.

But he was certain they *would* – the speed and realism of photography was here to stay, Kashiwara repeatedly said.

In the meantime, Kashiwara targeted new markets and focused upon *group* portraits. He sent notices to the local schools extolling the advantages of yearly photographs of *each* class of students – telling the school administrators they would provide the institution with a photographic historical record of past and present students, and they would also be available for the enjoyment of the students and their families. Wily Kashiwara wanted to capitalize upon the prevalent atmosphere of inter-school rivalry in Tokyo, and the fact that few parents would be able to resist the pleas of their children for a copy of the class photograph – year after year.

At the same time, Kashiwara's advertisements in a local newspaper began to target fraternal, religious, military and religious groups – who also responded enthusiastically to the idea of a group portrait. And lest a wedding ceremony simply generate a portrait of the bride and groom, Kashiwara promoted the idea of photographs of the entire wedding party and also the guests. Yes, Hamish's former apprentices assured him, Kashiwara had the commercial skill to promote photography with great success in Japan.

Hamish was happy to hear of the workshop's success – proud to have contributed by his introduction of photography into the woodcut print product line, and pleased to know the staff would likely have jobs for some years to come. Of course, during his contacts with Kashiwara and his staff, Hamish had to struggle to appear ignorant of their *underground* products. This was more difficult when talking with his former apprentices in the studio – than with

Kashiwara, because he could not erase the images of their engagement in sexual activities in the photographs Toshiro had shown him. It was impossible to look at them and not *see* their naked, aroused bodies in his mind's eye.

By the time Hamish accepted Kashiwara's invitation to dinner the night before he left for Yokohama, he was personally satisfied he had given his employer good value for the investment that had been made in bringing him from abroad.

As he sat at Kashiwara's Western-style dining table, in a Western-style chair, he was reminded how much he missed such comfort – after months of living, eating and sleeping on tatami-covered floors.

Hamish noted that the meal, served by Mr. and Mrs. Saigo, was composed of his favorite Japanese dishes, for which he showed enthusiastic approval. He had already set aside a substantial cash gratuity to give them on the morrow for all their kindnesses during his stay.

Kashiwara was subdued during that last dinner, as was the light conversation. He thanked Hamish again for the re-direction his skill had brought to his enterprise – in the form of new products and new markets, and appeared to be fully-satisfied with the expense involved in bringing Hamish to Japan from California. And for his part, Hamish expressed gratitude for the opportunity to experience this once-in-a-lifetime adventure in a foreign land.

Hamish was on edge, however, throughout the meal – fearful that Kashiwara would mention his failure to secure a portrait commission from Toshiro. But the subject, thankfully, was not raised. And since neither Kashiwara nor any of his staff had mentioned Toshiro's death, he assumed that sad event had not yet been made public by Hiro or Toshiro's family – but for how much longer?

By pre-arrangement, Mr. Saigo took Hamish to the Tokyo railway station early enough the next morning, so that he could return to transport Kashiwara to the workshop afterwards. Just as they were leaving the villa, Mrs. Saigo came forward and handed Hamish a small, plain, lacquered *bento box* – of the type sold in street markets for purchase by laborers and other workers of modest means. With her husband translating for her, she related it would provide him with lunch on the train to Yokohama.

At that moment, Hamish decided not to wait until they reached the railway station to give them a cash gift for all the courtesies shown him during his stay. He reached into one of his pockets and brought forth a more-than-generous packet of yen. As he handed it to *Mr.* Saigo, in keeping with local custom, he bowed and said "*Domo arigato*". They responded in kind, and Hamish thought he might have detected just a hint of tears forming in Mrs. Saigo's eyes.

At the Tokyo railway station, Mr. Saigo guided Hamish to the Yokohama train. The night before, when Kashiwara gave him his tickets for the train and ship, he also gave him a note written in Japanese to show the railway porters in Yokohama, to be sure he was safely directed to his lodging the night before his ship sailed. The note also directed porters at the inn, where he would be staying, to take him to the harbor well before embarkation for San Francisco.

On the train, Hamish opened the bento box and found four compartments respectively filled with rice, sushi, pickled vegetables and a sweet for dessert. He eagerly downed the meal, sadly cognizant that it was the last time he would taste Mrs. Saigo's cooking. Afterward, it occurred to him that the box was small enough to take back home in his luggage. He wasn't sure what he would do with it, but the thought crossed his mind that it might make a nice trinket-box to brighten Maisie's shabby room. But then he frowned at the thought of Morton Street, uncertain as to whether he would ever visit the bordello again, upon his return home. This remained an issue with which he had wrestled since the night he shared Toshiro's pallet, where he engaged in sexual acts hitherto unknown to him *and* unimagined. He reckoned he would have a great deal of time on the long voyage home to evaluate his recent attraction to Japanese men, and assess its implications for continued bordello visits.

As he stared at the bento box, uncertain of its destination – whether to Maisie's room or atop the small chest in the living quarters behind his studio, he realized it required cleaning and drying *before* he placed it in one of his trunks.

He signaled a train porter, pantomimed cleaning and drying the little compartments which had held the food – and offered several yen as an incentive to assist him. The porter bowed, smiled, took the box and rushed away. Before long, he returned with the box wiped clean of any food particles and dry to the touch.

As Hamish continued to view the passing scenery, he recalled his initial train trip in Japan – as he traveled from Yokohama to Tokyo shortly after he arrived, and an eventual adventure beyond anything he could have imagined that day.

As he watched the workers in the fields and rice paddies, he particularly enjoyed the unique Japanese scarecrows on view. They had puzzled him upon initial viewing months before, and when he mentioned that to Toshiro during one of their many conversations, the samurai explained that they were based upon *Zen* concepts. Their stylized, unrealistic design utilized bamboo, straw and sticks to merely create the outline of a person with a bow-and-arrow. The purpose, of course, was to scare off birds who might perceive that a *hunter* was in the area.

Eventually, the train arrived at Yokohama, and after Hamish tipped the train porter for removing his trunks and taking them to the entrance of the station, he showed him the note Kashiwara had prepared and the porter signaled to a group of independent laborers sitting nearby, anxious for work. Two of them saw to it that Hamish and his luggage were safely delivered to the inn where Kashiwara had made his reservation for that evening.

After the porters were paid and had departed, he stored his trunks in the tiny room that contained little more than a sleeping pallet. Then he wandered around Yokohama for a time, comparing it with the vastness and sophistication of Tokyo.

At nightfall, the innkeepers provided an evening meal, and soon he was sound asleep – assured beforehand he would be awaken early in the morning by the very conscientious, organized family which operated the small enterprise.

TWENTY-EIGHT

The next morning, Hamish stood next to his trunks on the Yokohama dock, as he watched the hustle-and-bustle around him. People were coming and going and objects were being carried on and off a variety of sea-going vessels – accompanied by the din of orders being shouted by ships' officers to their crews.

Hamish stared at the steamship which would take him back to San Francisco – a virtual *twin* of the one which had brought him to Japan. The name on the bow was different, but it was a replica of the other in appearance and structure – another wooden-hulled, paddlewheel, coal-fired vessel.

He was standing out of the way of the activity about him for the time being, having been told when he arrived that the *Cabin-Class* passengers and their luggage would be brought onboard first. And now, as his photographer's eye scanned the scene from this vantage point, he imagined many wonderful photographs in his mind's eye which he could have taken today – and regretted he could not do so.

The only objects, not generating noise within his visual range, appeared to be the *sampan* darting in and out among the larger vessels – as they headed out to sea where the fish were apparently more plentiful. Some were soon so far away that they and the fishermen aboard them appeared only as silhouettes on the horizon – beautiful images waiting to be captured on his glass plates and magically turned into objects of enjoyment for years to come, long after the sampan had deteriorated and the fishermen were dead.

His attention was once again turned back to the arriving passengers when a clamor of horse hoofs caused him to look in their direction. Two very fine, large black carriages pulled up near his ship's passenger entrance. In the first one, a middle-aged Japanese couple sat on one seat – opposite two young women sitting on the other. In the second carriage a young man, perhaps several years older than the young women, sat opposite three large trunks. At the same time, Hamish noted the mixture of clothing styles among these folks. Both men were dressed in Western-style, formal black suits, while the women were dressed in kimonos, with their hair and makeup in the Japanese fashion.

He couldn't prevent himself from wondering if this group was a family consisting of parents and their three children – or if the young man was the husband of one of the young women. But he soon was distracted from that thought when the young man left his carriage and went to the ship's officer who was checking the passenger list. After the requisite mutual bows, he handed him what had to be travel documents, which the ship's officer then compared with the list he held in his hand. When he was satisfied, the officer called over several dockside porters and instructed them to retrieve the trunks from the carriage and carry them onboard.

The young man then returned to the first carriage, offered his hand to assist the two young women as they stepped out, and then the three of them lined up facing the older couple. While the latter sat stiffly

• The Meiji Prince •

in their carriage, the young trio bowed low and long in their direction. In return they received a slight nod of the head from the older couple. And then the three passengers turned and walked onboard the ship, as the carriages slowly pulled away.

How odd, Hamish thought, as he compared this apparent family separation with the emotions openly exhibited under similar circumstances whenever he went to the San Francisco harbor to take photographs, or simply to exercise and enjoy the view. Americans under such circumstances did not hold back their feelings – hugging and weeping openly, without shame. But he had also been in Japan long enough to know full well that public displays of emotion were almost exclusively reserved for festivals, such as the one to which Toshiro and Hiro had taken him.

Later, once inside his Compartment, he quickly noted it was identical to that which he had inhabited on the voyage *to* Japan. And so once again, he stored his clothing trunk on the floor, underneath the lower bunk and next to the covered chamber pot. He then carefully used the lower bunk's pillow and blanket to stabilize and cushion the trunk which contained his precious camera, as it lay on that bunk. He would sleep in the upper bunk, where at night the incoming moonlight and starlight from the small glass porthole would help lessen the claustrophobic feeling of this confined space.

When the lunch bell was rung, he answered it promptly, rather hungry at the moment. And as on the other ship, he found an etched glass screen separating the dining galley into distinct areas, one for each of the two classes of passengers.

After lunch he went out to the Promenade and

sat in a deck chair, watching the Japanese mainland fade further and further in the distance. How he wished *some* of his memories of Japan would also fade as easily. But he knew he would likely wrestle throughout his lifetime with unanswered questions, such as, *Why did Toshiro kill himself, and in such a brutal manner?* Every time he found himself enjoying a fond memory of his samurai Sensei, he soon became enraged for having been made a party to the events of that terrible day. *Why did you expose me to it – by having me photograph that bloody ceremony, Sensei?*

Before dinner that evening, he decided to *finally* open the gift Toshiro had left for him – while there was still fading daylight coming through the porthole to supplement the dim light from the wall-mounted lamp. Much to his surprise, Toshiro had given him the beautiful blue-eyed tiger scroll, which had hung in his sleeping quarters!

Upon seeing it, Hamish started to tremble and sob, while at the same time being careful to hold the delicate scroll away from his falling tears. After he wiped away the tears, he rolled it up again, and returned it to the long box in which it had come. He then stored it in his clothing trunk, which also held the farewell gift from Kashiwara and his staff – as well as the bento box from Mrs. Saigo. He was uncertain as to whether he would be able to bring himself to hang it up in his cramped living quarters back home – knowing that every time he looked at it, there would be a flood of unsettling memories, and mixed emotions.

All night long, he tossed and turned restlessly, obsessed with the notion that *he* had been the *blue-eyed one* for whom Toshiro had so longed. And yet, Toshiro enjoyed Hamish's body and love-making for but a single evening – before slashing open his abdomen and then demanding to be beheaded, just several days later.

TWENTY-NINE

After his restless night, Hamish was in no mood to converse with his breakfast companions the following morning. On the previous day, when introductions were exchanged at table, he was careful to describe his reason for being in Japan as *personal business*, and happily no one pressed him further. He did experience a light moment upon entering the dining galley – discovering that after only *two* meals aboard ship, lunch and dinner the previous day, the other passengers had already staked out their seats at table. And as people are wont to do, they made clear they expected to occupy those same places for the rest of the journey.

After breakfast, he found the Promenade too crowded and noisy. He paused, trying to decide where to seek solitude other than in his cell-like Compartment. Previous visits to the Gymnasium on his earlier voyage had proven it to be a place of boisterous conversation and boasting of sexual exploits among the men who congregated there, and he was in no mood for any of that on this day. And so instead, he elected to go to the Library – hoping it would be quiet there.

Upon entering, he was relieved to find it unoccupied. As with the previous ship's Library, this one also had an assortment of English and Japanese-language reading materials, separated into groups at either end of a narrow table.

Hamish quickly spotted copies of *Harper's New Monthly Magazine* and *The Atlantic Monthly* – and hoped they were not the *same* issues he had read and re-read on the way to Japan. Happily, although rather dated, they were not the same issues. He quickly selected a copy of *Harper's* and sat down to read, in a comfortable chair.

He had only just begun to examine its contents when the door opened and a young Japanese gentleman entered. Hamish immediately recognized him as a member of the family party which had boarded the ship the day before. The young man promptly bowed to Hamish and greeted him with a cheerful, "Good Morning!"

Hamish felt obliged to rise from his chair, bow, and respond in Japanese – "*Ohayo Gozaimasu!*"

The young man appeared to appreciate the gesture. "So you speak Japanese, Sir?" He asked.

Hamish answered, "Only a few words, Sir." And then it occurred to him he had best attempt to fend off any questions about his time in Japan.

"I have been in your country for awhile, dealing with some personal matters, and only had time to learn a bit of your language."

Hamish counted on Japanese reticence and courtesy around strangers to prevent the young man from probing further, and his supposition proved to be correct. At the same time, Hamish was surprised to find that he was interested in continuing the conversation, despite his earlier desire for solitude.

"Can I ask where you learned English, Sir?"

The young man nodded. "My father hired a private tutor for me – he thought it would be good for business."

"Business?" Hamish replied.

"For several decades my family has been importing tea from China. And now, we are about to expand our product line – adding tea from Ceylon and Japan as well, and exporting it to America. This trip to San Francisco is for the purpose of establishing contacts with importers there."

By now, Hamish found himself so comfortable talking to the young man that all previous thoughts of solitude were set aside.

"I see," Hamish replied. "I wish you and your family good luck. Americans prefer *coffee*, I'm afraid to have to tell you – but the more genteel folks drink tea, and also those who are just plain rich. And there are some mighty wealthy people in San Francisco."

The other gentleman appeared lost in thought for a few moments, causing Hamish to worry that he might have said something discouraging. But then his fellow traveler smiled and walked over to the Japanese-language reading material on the table and picked up a newspaper. He then settled into a chair opposite Hamish.

Shortly, they were interrupted by the entrance of two young Japanese women wearing Western-style dresses and smoking cigarettes. They rushed over to the young man and excitedly twirled around several times, so he could get a full view of their attire. While doing so, they laughed and spoke excitedly in Japanese. And then, as suddenly as they had entered the room, they rushed out the door.

The young man observed the puzzled expression on Hamish's face and laughed softly.

"My sisters – they are not allowed to wear Western clothing at home. And so I am afraid they secretly visited a specialty shop in the Ginza – even I did not know about it at the time. Everything they purchased was then hidden, to be worn on this trip. This is the first time I have seen them without kimonos. Our honorable mother would be very displeased if she knew. And I should feel guilty to some extent, as I have been entrusted to be their guardian and chaperone – until we reach San Francisco. Once there, much to my relief, our honorable uncle and his wife will assume that responsibility."

Hamish now found himself increasingly intrigued, and eager to converse, despite his earlier reluctance.

"You have family in San Francisco?" He asked.

"Our honorable uncle is a member of the Japanese Counsel's staff there. We shall be staying with him, and his wife will tend to my sisters while I deal with my family's business venture."

Hamish deliberately chose *not* to inquire if Mr. Hasegawa was the uncle in question, out of fear he would have to explain the circumstances of their acquaintance. But he pressed on, unable for reasons unknown, to end the conversation.

"I believe I saw you and your family arrive at the dock yesterday. You and your father were dressed in Western-style clothing, but your mother and sisters wore kimonos. Can I ask why your family does not dress in the same style – or would that be rude of me?"

The young man appeared to grow serious in demeanor.

"Ah – pardon me for saying so, Sir, but you must have been in Japan for but a short while. My whole country is *divided* between those who think like my honorable mother – clinging to the past, and my honorable father and his kind who have eagerly embraced the direction the Meiji Government has taken since the fall of the Tokugawa Shogunate. I must admit, however, that as a young boy when the great change occurred, I was frightened – quite terrified for the future. And then, my honorable father helped me realize the inevitability of *change* in the human experience and the lack of control we have over much that occurs around us."

Hamish decided not to reveal the extent to which Toshiro had repeatedly made this schism clear to him, choosing to appear the naïve foreigner.

"Can I ask how he did that?"

"Yes – you may. It was really quite simple. He took me for a walk through the beautiful gardens of Ueno Park – have you been there? Of course, every visitor to Tokyo goes there! Anyway, he pointed to all the beautiful blossoms scattered about on the ground, beneath flowering trees and bushes. And then he recited an old adage:

> *It does not matter if the sign says*
> DO NOT PICK THE BLOSSOMS,
> *For the wind cannot read.*

And with that simple ancient proverb, I came to accept his admonition that there is much in life over which we have little control. I came to realize one must go along with the flow of history – which is little more than a record of inevitable *change* over time."

Hamish nodded, as if in agreement and then turned back to his magazine, as his companion turned to an *inside* page of the newspaper, which Hamish assumed dealt with business news. But then something on the front page of the Japanese newspaper, which the gentleman was holding in a manner that allowed Hamish to view it, caught his attention. It was an illustrative woodcut print, surrounded by

The Meiji Prince

Japanese writing. Even at a distance of several feet, the image appeared to be somewhat familiar.

Hamish leaned forward, pretending to re-tie the lace on one of his shoes, so he could get a closer look. When he did, he could no longer contain himself.

"Excuse me, Sir. Can I ask you what *that* is on the front page of your newspaper?"

The young man turned his attention to the front page, and studied it. "Oh, this is a woodblock print, used to illustrate the surrounding story."

"May I have a closer look, Sir? I grew mighty fond of your prints during my stay in Japan."

"Of course," the young man replied, as he passed the newspaper to Hamish.

Once he saw the print up close, Hamish *froze* in disbelief. It was clearly copied from the first photograph he had taken of Toshiro's seppuku ritual! It depicted a man kneeling before a small table upon which a bundle lay, and a single flower in a vase was on another small table to his right. While trying to conceal his shock Hamish asked, "Can you please tell me what this story is about?"

The other gentleman took back the newspaper, and silently studied it for what Hamish thought was an especially *long* time. Eventually, he spoke.

"This article reports the recent seppuku – ritual suicide, of the esteemed samurai, Master Toshiro. The print illustrates the start of the ceremony and the article indicates there was a second photograph taken *after* he was beheaded. The editor has chosen, for the sake of propriety, to show only this one – a print copied from its original photograph."

Now confused, as well as shocked, Hamish managed to ask, "Does the article tell *why* this samurai gentleman did such a thing?"

"Oh yes. It was apparently an act of defiance and protest against the Meiji Government. The article includes a Proclamation, which he ordered to be delivered to the editor, by his Page, along with the photographs – after his death. In it, he argues that the dissolution of the samurai class, and discouragement of other Japanese traditions, have all been for the worst. He disparages the movement toward Westernization and urges displeased former samurai to rise up in rebellion."

"Rebel against your Emperor? I believe he is *God* – isn't he?"

"Not against the Emperor – against the Western-oriented *Government*, which Toshiro believes is holding our Imperial Majesty against his will. Toshiro argues our Imperial Majesty is being forced to endorse and promote laws and edicts for modernization which are placed before him. He proposes the Emperor reluctantly agrees to do so, in order to ensure his personal safety and that of his family. Repeatedly, Toshiro's proclamation calls for the rejection of all things Western and foreign, and a return to a truly powerful, autonomous form of Imperial rule. And if necessary to accomplish this, he advocates open rebellion and bloodshed!"

Hamish became alarmed for the charming citizens of the nation he had just visited.

"Less than a decade ago, my country ended a terrible civil war. I would not visit such a horror upon *any* nation."

"Nor would I – but the reality is that nevertheless, it is well-known that former samurai are massing in isolated places to foment just such an action in the future. And we all live in fear of it."

"Does the samurai in the newspaper say anything else?"

"He just repeats several times the notion that his act of ritual suicide is to be taken as a public rejection of our nation's current path toward modernization and adoption of Western materialistic values – and for all loyal Japanese to join in the struggle."

And then, just as he prepared to lay aside the newspaper, Hamish's companion exclaimed, "Now *this* is interesting!"

Still shaken by what he had learned of Toshiro's suicide so far, Hamish sat up and leaned forward.

"This – see here, Sir, is an advertisement from the Kashiwara Studio."

Hamish squinted at a black-bordered area near the bottom of the front page, as the Japanese gentleman continued.

"According to this, the Kashiwara Studio had exclusive access to the original glass plates from which the photographs taken at Toshiro's seppuku were printed, and later rendered into woodblock prints by the newspaper."

"What?" Hamish exclaimed, too loudly and in a manner which he feared might have made the young man suspicious of his interest in the matter. However, his companion was apparently so absorbed in the advertisement that he paid little note, as he continued to speak.

"The Kashiwara people believe these photographs – of which there are but a limited number, will be in such great demand that they have not placed a price on them. Instead they will be sold at auction to the highest bidder…next week. Very interesting."

He then put down the newspaper, glanced at his

pocket watch and said to Hamish, "I believe I need to check upon my sisters. Please excuse me."

He rose and bowed, as did Hamish, and then left the Library. Now alone, Hamish stared at the woodblock print which had obviously been copied from one of *his* photographs. He was overwhelmed by what he had just learned, not knowing where or how to begin to unravel the unanswered questions now before him.

THIRTY

Hamish had no idea how long he remained in the ship's Library, transfixed by the woodblock print depicting the start of Toshiro's ritual suicide.

At some point, however, he found himself wandering out onto the Promenade, but the bright sun reflecting off the water and the conversations of people coming and going annoyed him. Reluctantly, he headed for his dark, but quiet, Compartment.

He lay upon the top bunk and stared at the low ceiling. The details related to him by the young Japanese gentleman, from the newspaper account of Toshiro's seppuku, were rolling around in his head. *Each* of the facts contained therein had implications – and he needed to sort them out in order to resolve his dilemma.

The task of doing so was proving to be overwhelming, until it occurred to him that perhaps he should apply the same orderly step-by-step process which he used when teaching apprentices the process of modern photography. And so, with *that* perspective as his guide, he first dealt with his feelings of having been *betrayed*.

Toshiro had alerted him earlier to Kashiwara's treachery – by leading Hamish to believe he was bringing him to Japan primarily to add photographic views of Tokyo and Japanese life to his postcard production line. His view that the public – both domestic and foreign, was expected to embrace this modern improvement over woodblock prints made perfect sense to Hamish. But from the day Toshiro had told him about Kashiwara's *underground* products, he felt guilty – as if he were somehow culpable in the matter of this *dirty business*.

However, by the time he boarded the ship for his return to San Francisco, he reconciled himself to the notion that he had no *direct* role in producing such items – and thus was able to largely absolve himself.

And even though Hamish was not highly educated in the formal sense, nor an intellectual by disposition – on some level he intuitively grasped the notion that perhaps the rapidly-developing inventions which heralded much of what was now called *modern*, might have unanticipated consequences for the human race. In regard to Japan in particular, he wondered if the Japanese people would eventually rue the day that Westerners showered them with their latest invention.

But while he was able to dismiss his anger at Kashiwara's betrayal – he still had to deal with Toshiro. The fact that Hiro had obviously been instructed to deliver copies of the photographs he had taken – and Toshiro's Proclamation, to the editor of a local newspaper suggested the use of his photographs to promote the samurai Master's political agenda had been planned well in advance. *But how far in advance?*

The worst interpretation Hamish would allow himself to put upon Toshiro's actions – in betraying him in the manner that he did, was that Toshiro had planned to do so *before* their first meeting. This led him to assume it was always Toshiro's plan to have Hamish one day photograph his seppuku. If Hamish accepted this notion, then he had been but a *tool* to be used by the wily samurai to eventually publicize his cause, after death.

But could Toshiro have been so cold and calculating? Was his sending Hiro to Kashiwara's studio for a portrait simply a ruse which allowed him to be invited later to Toshiro's villa, under the guise of discussing his Page's portrait? And while there, and on subsequent visits, did Toshiro carefully cultivate his friendship and trust – by offering him gracious hospitality and fascinating lessons on Japanese history and culture?

To accept such a premise would have meant to acknowledge he was but a *pawn* in Toshiro's grand final gesture – and not a *genuine* friend. And Hamish recognized *this* would represent an even greater betrayal than Kashiwara's.

He was wrestling with this issue when the bell was rung, indicating lunch was being served. He forced himself off his bunk and slowly walked to the dining galley. At table, he remained silent, unless someone spoke directly to him, and afterward returned to his Compartment.

As he looked around the confined space, he decided he could not spend another minute there – he needed fresh air and sunshine. And so he retrieved a large cap from his clothing trunk, pulled it well down over his forehead and upper face – and headed for the Promenade. Once there, he dragged a deck chair to a remote area – away from foot traffic, and sat down. His cap obscured most of his face and made it appear as if he might be sleeping – as passengers often did on the deck chairs, even though it did allow him a narrow view of the ocean as it passed by. Now he was ready to address the *next* issue on his list of troubling events.

The newspaper article made clear that Kashiwara had somehow gotten his hands on Hamish's glass plates – but how and when? He could not believe that Toshiro instructed Hiro to deliver them to the bogus *Prince*, for whom he clearly had little respect. The notion that he would have allowed Kashiwara to gain financially from his death was unthinkable! And Hiro certainly would *not* have dishonored his Master in such a way – even for personal financial profit.

Hamish paused for a moment to think of Hiro, who after castigating *him* as someone who did not have the fortitude to put duty above emotion – revealed his personal agony at having exhibited that very shortcoming when he delayed the release from agonizing pain that Toshiro's sword promised. Hamish could not help feeling sympathy for the devoted young Page, who would likely spend the rest of his life haunted by Toshiro's *second* cry for a merciful, swift death.

No – Hiro would not have betrayed Toshiro to Kashiwara, but who else could have? Suddenly, Hamish's attention turned to the only other person present on that fateful day – Mr. Ohsugi. He knew of Toshiro's seppuku *and* the fact that it had been photographed by Hamish. *But why and how could Mr. Ohsugi have used this information to his advantage?*

Despite his being a plain-spoken person, not well-versed in, nor prone to guile, it took Hamish but a short while to develop a scenario which he believed made infinite sense.

In view of Mr. Ohsugi's status in Toshiro's household, as a once-proud samurai now reduced to the position of household servant, Toshiro's suicide must have been devastating for him. Certainly, he mourned the death of his Master – while at the same time proud that the latter had upheld the noble Japanese tradition of seppuku. But on the other hand, Ohsugi's future was now at risk, filled with uncertainty over the knowledge that Toshiro had legitimate heirs in Kyoto who were likely to seize his estate as soon as possible. *In such a situation, where would he have turned?*

As far as Hamish knew, Mr. Ohsugi had but one close relative – a grandson who worked for.....Kashiwara! *Of course – he would have rushed from Toshiro's villa as soon as he could get away from Hiro, to inform his grandson of Toshiro's death and seek refuge in his home.*

Surely, Hamish surmised, when Mr. Ohsugi told his grandson what had transpired, the professional printer that he was would have recognized the value of the photographs taken by Hamish. *But was there any evidence he had convinced his grandfather to offer this information to Kashiwara – hopefully for a reward, in view of his now-precarious financial situation?*

Hamish was momentarily perplexed by this question, until he recalled Hiro's having told him that Ohsugi had been given a pushcart by Kashiwara, from which to sell the workshop's postcards in Ueno Park. *Of course! Obviously, it was his reward for passing on this valuable information. But then, how did Kashiwara get the plates away from him*, Hamish wondered – *long enough to make the auction prints?*

Soon, everything else fell into place in Hamish's mind. He recalled how, on the day after Toshiro's seppuku – just as he finished developing the two sets of prints his Sensei had requested, Mr. Saigo rushed him to the workshop at Kashiwara's request. On the way there, Hamish was both confused because Tuesday was not a *scheduled* workshop day for him, *and* concerned that he was being prevented from delivering the glass plates and the photographs promptly to Hiro, as promised.

It didn't take Hamish long to realize that the sudden *departure party* – almost ten days *before* he sailed, had been but a ruse to lure him away from his studio at the villa. In his absence, Kashiwara likely sent loyal staff members there, with instructions to develop as many photographs as possible while Hamish was being plied with sake at the party given in his honor.

In hindsight, Hamish surmised Kashiwara's goal was to incapacitate him, rendering him into a stupor which would lead to his having to spend the night sleeping in his Office. *And who better to surreptitiously develop the photographs in his absence than the two assistants he had trained and who he noted, in passing, were absent from the party?*

Hamish shook his head slowly from side-to-side, beneath his cap. *Kashiwara may have been a charlatan, despised by the Imperial Family and others for his pretensions – but he was undoubtedly a brilliant one!*

For a time, Hamish sat as motionless as possible, looking at the water through the narrow slit of visibility afforded by the cap, which hid half his face from view. A few passersby apparently assumed he was asleep, for no one disturbed him.

But there was *one* more troublesome issue he had to address, and even though he knew no one nearby could possibly *read* his mind, he still felt compelled to return to the privacy of his Compartment – where he would face the matter directly.

Within minutes he was lying on his back in the upper bunk, once again staring at the low ceiling above him. In this position he began to review his adult sexual history, such as it was.

He had left for Japan knowing that his monthly visits to Maisie had become routine – little more than a momentary release in the arms of a warm body. But he had *never* felt himself attracted to men nor the male form, in the past. In fact, as his modest business grew, and photography became more commonplace and desired, he found himself occasionally contemplating finding a wife and raising a family one day. After all, that was the path chosen by Boyd men for as long as anyone could remember.

But then, he encountered *Toshiro*, who over time told him of the longstanding history of love between men, in Japan – and most particularly among the samurai class. Gradually, Toshiro also introduced him to the spread of such a notion among the writings of renown scholars, poets – and even military and religious leaders. And as if that were not enough, he took him to the raucous festival where he observed dozens of half-naked and fully-naked men – many of whom cavorted in the most erotic fashion. And as a result, he was driven to a barely-concealed frenzy of lust that day, which had to be *relieved* as soon as he returned to his quarters at Kashiwara's villa.

This *indoctrination* to the strange world of man-love disoriented him and the way in which he thought about himself and his future. And then, Toshiro made aggressive, passionate love to him – the culmination of this extraordinary experience.

When he returned to his quarters that fateful Saturday morning, after Toshiro kissed him *Goodbye,* somewhere deep in his heart he hoped there would be at least one more such encounter during his remaining days in Japan. But of course, Monday's events put a note of finality upon any such fantasy.

And now, thanks to Toshiro, his head was filled

with confusion, his heart with disquiet – and his life-plan disrupted. At the moment, he found himself not knowing whose arms he desired to lay within – a man's or a woman's? And he dreaded returning home in such a state of bewilderment.

On the one hand, he feared that in any woman's arms he would now feel Toshiro's presence, and the powerful spell he held over him during their night of ecstasy. But on the other, seeking a substitute lover among the men of San Francisco would be too risky to contemplate. Eastern publishers, in their editorials which eventually reached the West Coast, still referred to the place as a *rough-and-tumble town – a part of the Wild West.* In such an environment he could not imagine finding even one man willing to engage in the intimacy he enjoyed on Toshiro's pallet. *And was that really what he desired in the long run, after all?*

At some point he fell asleep, exhausted by the stress he had been undergoing since shortly after he entered the ship's Library, following breakfast that morning. During his nap, he dreamt – his dreams a crazy-quilt of ideas and images prompted by the day's events. Toshiro, Kashiwara, Hiro, Saigo, and Ohsugi all appeared, disappeared and re-appeared – as his mind presented him with one frightening or confusing vision after another.

He awoke in late afternoon, and even before looking at his pocket watch, he could estimate the hour from the position and luminosity of the sunlight coming through the small porthole.

He lay still, waiting for the call to dinner. He awoke with a resolve to address directly the emotional pain and regret which now filled his heart and mind. His adventure in Japan had left him feeling betrayed by his employer *and* his intimate friend, having been used by both to their respective advantage. His final effort – the photographs of Toshiro's seppuku, had been expropriated for financial gain by one undeserving of such profit. And the other obviously desired them to publicize his political agenda – with Hamish as a pawn in the process.

And so he quietly waited, and listened intently for the call to dinner and the departure of his fellow passengers as they made their way to the dining galley. At mealtime, most of the crew also went there, to serve at table and take turns eating. It was crucial for him *not* to be seen when he went out to what he hoped would be a *deserted* Promenade. The *last* thing he wanted was for loud cries of *Man Overboard*, when impact with the sea created a loud splash, indicating a watery grave awaited.

Soon, the dinner bell rang, and the corridor leading to the Compartments emptied, as passengers walked past his door on their way to dinner. When he thought it was safe, he removed his camera and tripod from the trunk in which they were stored, and mounted the former securely atop the latter. He opened the door slowly and made his way to the Promenade – repeatedly checking for the presence of others.

It occurred to him that if he went to the area closest to the paddlewheel, the noise it made might mask the loud splash he expected when contact with the water was made. Once there, he looked about nervously one more time, and then swiftly tipped the tripod, camera-end first, over the railing – and with one strong push shoved it toward the deep, dark roaring sea.

He was relieved to discover that the paddlewheel noise did, in fact, cover the splashing sound. And he was even more delighted when no one came running, in a response to the noise.

Soon, he was back on the upper bunk in his Compartment, staring once again at the low ceiling. Part of his exhausted mind was telling him he had now *closed* the door on Japan, the reason he went there, and the distressful memories with which he had been left. But soon, another set of feelings and questions flooded his consciousness, as he wondered how in God's name he would now earn a living when he returned to the land of his birth?

THE END

CPSIA information can be obtained at www.ICGtesting.com
Printed in the USA
LVOW07s2201301014

411366LV00001B/48/P